PUFFIN

RANDOM ACTS

VALERIE SHERRARD has written more than a dozen novels for young people, including *Counting Back from Nine*, shortlisted for the Governor General's Award, and *The Glory Wind*, winner of the Geoffrey Bilson and Ann Connor Brimer Awards. Her work has been shortlisted for numerous Canadian awards, including CLA Book of the Year for Children, TD Canadian Children's Literature, Red Maple, and Snow Willow. She lives in Miramichi, New Brunswick.

Also by Valerie Sherrard

Counting Back from Nine

Rain Shadow

Driftwood

The Glory Wind

Tumbleweed Skies

Testify

Accomplice

Watcher

Speechless

Three Million Acres of Flame

Sarah's Legacy

Sam's Light

Kate

The Shelby Belgarden Mysteries

RANDOM ACTS

Valerie
Sherrard

PUFFIN

an imprint of Penguin Canada Books Inc., a Penguin Random House Company

Published by the Penguin Group
Penguin Canada Books Inc., 90 Eglinton Avenue East, Suite 700, Toronto, Ontario, Canada M4P 2Y3

Penguin Group (USA) LLC, 375 Hudson Street, New York, New York 10014, U.S.A.
Penguin Books Ltd, 80 Strand, London WC2R 0RL, England
Penguin Ireland, 25 St Stephen's Green, Dublin 2, Ireland (a division of Penguin Books Ltd)
Penguin Group (Australia), 707 Collins Street, Melbourne, Victoria 3008, Australia
(a division of Pearson Australia Group Pty Ltd)
Penguin Books India Pvt Ltd, 11 Community Centre, Panchsheel Park, New Delhi – 110 017, India
Penguin Group (NZ), 67 Apollo Drive, Rosedale, Auckland 0632, New Zealand
(a division of Pearson New Zealand Ltd)
Penguin Books (South Africa) (Pty) Ltd, 24 Sturdee Avenue, Rosebank,
Johannesburg 2196, South Africa

Penguin Books Ltd, Registered Offices: 80 Strand, London WC2R 0RL, England

First published 2015

1 2 3 4 5 6 7 8 9 10 (RRD)

Manufactured in the U.S.A.

LIBRARY AND ARCHIVES CANADA CATALOGUING IN PUBLICATION

Sherrard, Valerie, author
Random acts / Valerie Sherrard.

ISBN 978-0-14-319104-9 (pbk.)

I. Title.

PS8587.H3867R35 2015   jC813'.54   C2014-904174-8

eBook ISBN 978-0-14-319440-8

Visit the Penguin Canada website at **www.penguin.ca**

Special and corporate bulk purchase rates available; please see
www.penguin.ca/corporatesales or call 1-800-810-3104.

For my granddaughter Emilee.
Let your life sing.

One

Looking back, I blame the Buffalo wings the most.

I forget who decided it was a good idea to order what the local pizzeria calls the Friends' Combo. As in, a party pizza, garlic cheese fingers, a large Caesar salad, a dozen Buffalo wings, two litres of Pepsi and a tub of chocolate mint ice cream. We scarfed down every last crumb in about fifteen minutes, chomping and grunting like steroid-frenzied pigs at a trough. There were three of us.

The end result was a trio of sad faces on top of bloated bodies—sprawled attractively in my living room—clothes loosened, immobilized by our own gluttony. The overdose made me drowsy but there was a lot of whimpering in the air and that prevented me from dozing off.

And yes, some of those moans came from me, but the loudest came from the exaggerated performance of Bean, whose real name is Emerson Firth. The nickname is courtesy of his grandmother, who called him "Butter Bean" when he was a baby. After that, it went through a few adaptations as he grew, including Beanski, Beaner and Beanbo, before it slimmed down to plain old Bean. Ironically, the one (and only) person who calls him Emerson now is that same grandmother.

Bean was nearly horizontal in Dad's old green recliner—the ugliest but also most comfortable chair in the room. His glasses were kind of skewed on his face, which made him look a bit less geek-like than usual. With short dark hair, a thin triangular face and glasses, Bean can't escape the geek label. Everyone expects him to be able to solve their computer problems or help them with their math, when the truth is it took him an hour to master his iPhone. Seriously.

Not that he's dumb. That's not what I'm trying to say at all. He might even be a bit above average in some things, but he's no genius. He just looks like one.

The second person suffering from the Italian overdose that day was Jenna Bayley. Jenna is my other best friend, and an organization freak.

Schedules and lists are kind of an obsession with her. I swear she goes through at least one notebook and a whole pad of Post-it Notes a week—even though she has everything stored electronically and backed up to the yin-yang. At any given time, I can find a dozen or more notes from her in my possession. Here are a few examples of the important things Jenna feels the need to write down, even though nine times out of ten she's already sent me a text saying the same thing:

I'll be over at 7:00.
Hey, Zoey! Check out Surprised Kitty on YouTube.
Don't forget to download the RunKeeper app.

I think you get the idea.

We're your quintessential practically-thirteen-year-olds, Jenna and I. Both of us are oh-so-ordinary, never-going-to-stand-out-in-a-crowd types, although she's the skinny version and I have my struggles with various bulges. We both wear our hair (hers is dark blond while mine is boring brown) long and straight. I have bangs and she doesn't.

Jenna's post-piggery pose was, frankly, a bit annoying. She was sprawled across the couch with her jeans unzipped and her super-stuffed tummy protruding approximately a quarter of an inch. For *that*, you need to unzip?

It didn't exactly flood my heart with sympathy as she lay there muttering things like, "I'm dying," and "Why'd I do it?"

"Why'd you do *what*?" Bean asked. "Nearly take my arm off over the last piece of pizza?"

"No. Why'd I *eat* so much," Jenna groaned.

"You don't see a connection between the two things?" Bean said.

"Shut up, Bean." Jenna swatted the air, as if her arm might magically reach across the room.

But Bean's focus had shifted. A faraway look crept over his face as he lifted his right leg several inches. His butt rose from the chair and hung suspended, rather menacingly I might add, in the air.

Jenna bolted upright. "Do NOT do that in here!" she yelled.

"What? You want me to swell up until I burst and die?" Bean asked. He actually tried to look offended as he lowered himself back into the chair.

"Yes, Bean. That's exactly what I want. To be in a room with your bloated corpse," Jenna said.

"It won't be bloated if it bursts," Bean pointed out.

"Even more appealing," Jenna said. "Could you *try* not to be so gross!"

"I'm a *guy*," he said, like that was a legitimate excuse.

In the interests of full disclosure, I should mention that last year this particular guy was my sort-of boyfriend. Sort-of because I'm not officially allowed to have a boyfriend yet. Thankfully, that torturous part of my romantic history (actually, that *is* my romantic history) is over. After a wretched summer of what amounted to some sweaty handholding and a couple of awkward kisses, we broke up. Our romance was so ill-fated that even the breakup was an accident.

Bean thinks *I* called it quits, which isn't actually the case. We were on the phone one day around the end of August and I was flipping through the programming menu on the TV when the remote suddenly refused to co-operate. I tapped it against my hand a few times.

"Oh, come on!" I said.

"What?" Bean asked.

"This isn't working," I grumbled.

"Oh, thank goodness!" Bean said before I could explain that I was talking about the remote. "I've wanted to say that for ages but I didn't have the courage."

I stopped fiddling with the remote. "Right,

well—" Since I didn't have a clue what he was talking about, I left it at that and waited for a hint of some sort. It didn't take long.

"When did you know?" His voice was animated, like when you're super-excited about something. Luckily, he was too thrilled to wait for me to answer. "I think *I* knew almost right away, but I kept trying to talk myself out of it, or into it, or whatever. But let's face it—going out was … just … *weird*. Only, I didn't know what to do about it."

There was a pause. By then, I'd gotten it. My boyfriend was in a rapturous fit over the thought that I was dumping him. It's hard to know what to say in that kind of situation.

"Anyway, Zoey," Bean went on, "the important thing is that we're admitting it now. I didn't say anything before because I was scared we'd stop being friends. That would be horrible."

"Awful!" I said. It *would* be horrible not to be friends with Bean.

"But this is *perfect*," he said. "Now that we know we both feel the same, we can go back to the way it was before we had this crazy idea."

All true, and yet I couldn't help feeling put out. I managed to hide my annoyance and act like I was just as happy as he was. And once it sank in, I honestly was. Dating Bean had been a mess, start to finish. After being close friends since approximately forever, going out had *seemed* like a great idea. Except it wasn't. It was as if all the ease and comfort had disappeared from our friendship, and the effort of *pretending* to be happy nearly wore me out.

That was a year ago. And ever since we broke up it's been fine.

Also since the breakup, I, Zoey Dalton, incredibly average grade seven student and only child of divorced parents, have remained single.

I live with my dad, a psychologist who operates a private practice called Therapy Solutions. It's not what you'd call conventional counselling. The brochure describes it as "Healing Through Primitive Dance and Expression."

"My clients learn how to nurture *themselves*," Dad is fond of explaining. "I teach them self-awareness and acceptance through the beauty of movement and primordial communication."

Bean calls it the Wail and Flail Club, although it's actually pretty progressive here in the small town of Breval, Ontario. (That's a made-up name, because my dad's clients deserve their privacy. They have enough problems without everyone knowing their business.) I work at Therapy Solutions, which makes me the only practically-thirteen-year-old around with a real

job. A few months ago Dad's regular receptionist, Gina Barducci, apparently noticed she
had no life and decided she didn't want to work
evenings any more.

To be honest, I didn't quite see what
someone her age would need all that free time
for. Miss Barducci is at least forty—she should
have realized that if her Romeo hasn't shown up
yet, he probably isn't going to. But maybe she
just wanted more time to play with her cats, or
whatever it is old maids do these days.

Whatever her reasons, it was a perfect
opportunity for me to make some money. My
allowance never lasts even half the week, and
Dad doesn't believe in topping it up unless it's
for something *he* thinks is important.

Well, it took days and days of *relentless*
pestering to persuade him that I was mature
enough to handle the job. (Don't ask me what the
big deal is about sitting at a desk and answering
the phone.) It's only four hours a week—two
each on Tuesday and Thursday evenings—and
since I'm too young to be an official employee,
Dad pays me cash. Sweet.

The patients are interesting, that's for sure.
These people need a *way* different kind of help
than they'd ever get lying on a couch and telling
someone about their childhood.

Coincidentally, helping people was the subject that led to our plan the day we ate ourselves into an Italian stupor.

The food-induced daze is real, by the way. Apparently, your stomach uses extra oxygen when it's digesting a heavy, fatty meal. This causes a shortage to other parts of the body, including the brain. Which, of course, is why those Buffalo wings deserve most of the blame for what happened when Jenna's phone blasted out the sound of bubble wrap popping. Jenna's taste in ringtones is questionable at best.

"FaceTime request from Destiny," she announced as she accepted the call. I snuck a peek at Bean, who had sprung an instant frown. No surprise there.

If there's one person Bean cannot *stand*, it's Destiny Desotto. It's silly, really. He's been that way since she yanked down his shorts in gym back in grade three. It caused quite a scandal, as far as scandals go in elementary school. The story raced through the hallways that he'd had skid-marks on his underwear. Bean has always insisted that he accidentally put his briefs on backwards that morning. According to him, the dark lines were nothing more sinister than trim for the "access area." Since that version of events was boring, everyone ignored it. He never forgave Destiny.

Jenna had hardly said hello to the smiling face on her screen when Destiny launched into the reason for her call.

"Hey, Jenna!" She squinted, seeing my face peering at her over Jenna's shoulder. "Hey, Zoey! Cool—you're both there. I wanted to tell you about this new club I'm starting. It's called Lend a Hand—and it's just what you'd expect from the name. We do good deeds—help people out, that sort of thing."

"Is this a new school club?" I asked.

"Well, it's mostly kids from school, but it's *my* group. I started it with a few close friends, but we thought we'd spread out and invite others to join."

"What kinds of things do you do?" Jenna asked.

"The list is endless, really. Volunteer dog-walking, collecting for the food bank, doing small jobs and errands for people who need help ... I could go on."

"Sounds like it takes a *lot* of organizing," Jenna said, unable to keep the excitement out of her voice. Poor thing.

"It does, but I do a pretty good job managing that myself."

"You mean you send out your minions and then make sure you get the credit?" Bean asked from behind me.

Destiny frowned. "Is that Bean?" she asked.

"Yes," Jenna said.

"Maybe I should call back later."

"Why?" Bean asked. "Because I hit a nerve?"

"It's not about getting credit," Destiny said, "but then you never do anything for anyone except yourself, so I doubt you can actually grasp the concept."

"I do things for people," Bean said, which wasn't strictly true. Or even remotely true.

"Look, I have to go," Destiny said. She put her bright smile back on. "If you two are interested, let me know. Bean, of course, isn't someone we'd want in the group even if he *did* want in."

There was a kind of silence for a second after the screen went black. Then Bean said, "Oh, *no!* I'm not wanted!"

"That wasn't called for," Jenna said. "And if that's the way she wants to treat Bean, she can forget about any of us joining."

"Right," I agreed. "It's not like we were interested anyway."

Jenna gave me an odd look.

"What?" I said.

"I *liked* the idea."

"Seriously?" Bean and I said together.

"What? Is there something wrong with wanting to do things for other people?"

"It's not like we *never* help anyone," I said.

"Are you *kidding* me? We barely do things for *each other*."

"Yeah, but it's not like we only care about ourselves," Bean said. "We're just lazy."

"Great defence, Bean," Jenna said.

"So, do your own good deeds if it's such a big deal to you," Bean told her.

"It's not the same as being part of a group."

"Start your own group, then," I said.

"So everyone would think I was copying Destiny? Tell me that wouldn't be the lamest thing ever," Jenna said.

"You could keep it a secret," Bean said. I'm almost positive he was being sarcastic, but if he was, Jenna missed it.

"That's perfect! So, are you guys in?" She looked back and forth between us. Her face was happy and hopeful—not the kind of face you want to disappoint.

"I guess," Bean said. If he felt any actual enthusiasm for the idea, he hid it well.

"Sounds good to me," I said, hoping I sounded more sincere than Bean. "So—what now?"

Jenna leapt to her feet. "I know! We'll do random acts of kindness!" she shouted.

"Random ... what?" Bean asked.

"Acts of kindness," Jenna said. "We'll do nice things for people, only we'll do them anonymously, like we talked about."

"Huh," I said, while Bean made a similarly enthusiastic grunting sound.

Jenna's eyes narrowed. She looked back and forth at me and Bean.

"Forget it," she said. Her lower lip trembled. "It's obvious neither of you really wants to do this."

"I *said* I'd do it. Anyway, it probably won't be *that* lame," Bean said. He can't handle female pouting. He claims it makes him feel like he's holding his breath.

"Yeah, it'll be great," I said.

Jenna perked right back up.

"We'll call it the Random Acts club," she said. "And the *best* thing is, it will just be the three of us."

"Why?" I asked.

"Because, silly—it's a secret club. If you invited someone else and they didn't want to do it, they could tell people. But it's perfect this way—it'll be our own thing."

And you know what? It *did* sound kind of cool when she put it that way. So what if I wasn't as enthusiastic as Jenna? It wasn't going to hurt to get behind the idea if it was important to her. Besides, I figured it would be something we could all be proud of someday.

I figured wrong.

Two

We decided to meet at Bean's place the next day—to plan and organize the details. (I don't think I have to tell you whose suggestion *that* was.) I was the last one to get there, which was my dad's fault. He picked the exact moment I was about to leave to put his foot down about the state of my room. He does that a few times a year when, as he says, the joke has gone far enough. Whatever that means.

"Can't I do it later? I have a really important meeting," I told him.

"What kind of meeting?"

"It's, uh, kind of a secret."

"Well, it's no secret that your bedroom looks like a disaster zone. I'm afraid you're not going anywhere until it's cleaned up."

I stomped to my room and hurled dirty

clothes into the hamper like a madwoman. Then I raced around with the vacuum in one hand and the duster in the other, kicked a few things under the bed and shoved others into the closet.

It looked a lot better, which was all that really mattered. I tiptoed through the house and then paused, with one foot out the back door, to yell, "My room's done! Bye!"

Ten minutes later I was at Bean's house, ringing the doorbell. His mom answered it with her usual bubbly greeting.

"Zoey! Honey! You just bring yourself on in here!"

I was already inside, but I said thanks and steeled myself for the hug I knew was coming. Bean's mother has acted like I'm some kind of walking, talking cry for affection ever since my parents got divorced a couple of years ago.

"Now, where's my hug?"

Right on schedule. I endured the unnecessarily long squeeze *and* the accompanying sounds—monkey-like "Mmm, Mmm, Mmm, Mmm, Mmm" noises that rose and fell in pitch as she wound down to let go.

"It's *always* so good to see you, Zoey."

"Uh, thanks. It's nice to see you too, Mrs. Firth." I forced a smile while I edged away. "Is Bean around?"

"He sure is, honey. He's downstairs with Jenna."

"Thanks." I hurried down the steps and into the Firth Family Room. (Yes, that's actually what it's called—there's a sign over the door and everything. So lame.)

Bean and Jenna looked up as I dropped into a chair. "Sorry I'm late," I told them. "Dad got on my case about my room and I had to stop and clean it before I came over."

"Wow. It's a wonder you made it here at all," Bean said.

"It's not that bad."

"Are you kidding? We found *mould* growing in there once—remember?"

"That was on a piece of bread that had fallen under the bed," I said.

"Things don't fall *under* the bed," Bean said.

"Maybe it bounced … or rolled under."

"My mistake," Bean said. "It must have been a *ball* of bread, then, was it? Or a hunk of some kind of rubber loaf?"

"Not necessarily," Jenna said. "Maybe the laws of physics cease to exist in Zoey's room."

"That's right," I said. "Something like *your* room, Jenna, where pillows can magically transform themselves into—"

"Ancient history," she blurted, cutting me

off. "Anyway, now that you're *finally* here, how about we get down to business?"

"Sure."

Jenna glanced down at some notes she'd made and said, "I did a little research—to get some ideas for the kinds of things we could do."

Bean looked bored already.

"A lot of the suggestions I saw cost money, or couldn't be done secretly. We'll be better off coming up with our own ideas."

"Sounds okay to me," I said.

"Hey, what if we do something that's not exactly *nice*, but it's for someone's own good?" Bean asked. The thought seemed to cheer him.

"Bean!" Jenna swatted his shoulder. He grinned and shrugged, because of course he isn't that dumb. He was just trying to get Jenna riled up.

"Anyway, I kind of did up a contract for us to sign," Jenna admitted. She didn't look at either Bean or me when she said it.

"Seriously?" I asked. Some things are hard to believe even when you know they're true. Now and then I wonder if Jenna's obsession with organizing might be some kind of actual disorder. (I am, after all, the daughter of a psychologist. I probably inherited some kind of analyzing gene.)

Bean and I leaned forward and looked at the contract she'd done up. It had a seal and fancy lettering across the top and a bunch of "therefore"s and "wherefore"s and "hereafter"s throughout. I skimmed it, took the pen she was holding out to me and signed my name.

Okay, it wasn't a huge deal—a few words on a piece of paper. I know that, so I can't quite explain the feeling it gave me. Like I'd just done something noble and important.

I turned toward Bean and Jenna wondering if they were feeling it too—proud and a little soppy and almost (but not quite, since I'm not a moron) heroic.

Bean stared vacantly ahead and let out a long belch. Just about as much emotional depth as you'd expect from him.

Jenna, on the other hand, was looking at me with a trembling smile and shining eyes.

I was going to say something to her, and it probably would have been something meaningful that we'd remember years from now, but my phone rang at that exact minute.

I glanced at the display and felt a jolt go through me.

Dennis Fuller!

I blinked. I looked again. His name was still there.

Dennis Fuller—gorgeous, smart, funny. The perfect combination of good guy/bad boy, with just enough edge in there to make him interesting.

Dennis Fuller, who had never called me before—who I'd never even talked to long enough to call it an actual conversation. (Well, there was that one time we were in the same group for a Biology project, but that was last year, and besides, anything school-related doesn't count.)

Dennis, with brown eyes that are so dark and deep they're nearly black.

When my heart started beating again, I pulled myself together and answered.

"Hi—is this Zoey?" he asked.

"Yes it is," I said. I used a coolly sophisticated tone so he'd know a phone call from a nearly perfect guy was nothing new to me.

"Zoey, this is Dennis."

Bean and Jenna were looking at me curiously. I put a finger to my lips to signal them to be quiet. Bean took this as a prompt to do the exact opposite, but Jenna, seeing the frantic look on my face, stepped up. She clapped one hand over Bean's mouth and used the other one to twist his right arm behind his back—just enough to let him know she wasn't letting him mess up my call. (And probably so she could eavesdrop more easily, but whatever.) When there's a job to be done, Jenna does not fool around.

"Hi, Dennis. What's up?" I slipped down to a warm, sultry sound.

Jenna's eyes popped open wider. (Bean's were already good and wide, but I'm pretty sure that was from the shock of Jenna's attack.) She mouthed, *Dennis who?*

I held up a finger and shifted my attention back to the phone in time to catch what Dennis said next.

"I was wondering if you've heard about the new Lend a Hand group."

"I sort of heard something," I said, keeping it vague.

He gave me a few details and ended by saying, "Sounds like a good thing to do. And it shouldn't take up a whole lot of time."

"That's true," I said, ramping up the sultry. So what if he *wasn't* calling to talk about how long he's secretly been crushing on me? It wouldn't hurt to plant a few subliminal thoughts in his head with my sexy voice.

"So, you're in?" he said.

"Can I think about it and call you back?" I asked. I think on my feet like that—creating an excuse to call him back. It would give me time to plan a few interesting and witty things to say, too, since my head seemed a touch blank just then.

"Yeah, no problem," he said. "Give me a call when your cold is better." Apparently, my sultry tone of voice needed work.

Jenna let Bean go as I slipped the phone back into my bag. Bean rubbed his arm and gave her a sulky look. She ignored him and turned to me.

"Was that Dennis *Fuller?*" she asked.

"Yeah."

"Well? What did he want?"

"Oh, nothing, really," I said.

"He called you for no reason?" Jenna's hands were on her hips and she looked more than a little suspicious.

"I heard you say you'd call him back," Bean said accusingly.

"Right, because I couldn't follow what he was saying—thanks to all the commotion you were making in the background."

Jenna punched Bean on the shoulder. "See? Now we don't know what the guy wanted, and it's all your fault."

I joined her in glaring at Bean but the truth was, my mind was racing. Even if it was about Destiny's group, Dennis had called me himself— obviously that meant something. I didn't want to betray Bean and Jenna by joining Lend a Hand, but I didn't want to miss a chance for Dennis to see me as more than just another girl from school either.

It took me less than a minute to decide that there really wouldn't be any harm in joining Lend a Hand *and* doing random acts of kindness.

Three

The first random act I decided to do was to help the Kimuras, an elderly couple who live three houses down on our street. I don't know exactly how old they are, but my guess is they've passed their expiration dates. His face is puckered like an apple that's wizened and dried out, while hers is a mass of wrinkles that droop down around her chin and jaw. They're both so frail and bony you'd almost expect them to blow away in a strong wind, and they walk bent over, shuffling, like they dropped something and they're looking for it.

The Kimuras get the same paper we do, and our new paperboy has really lousy aim. When I go by their place on my way to school the paper is always on their walkway, or somewhere on the lawn, or almost anywhere *except* on the veranda where it's supposed to be.

I've seen Mr. Kimura retrieving it, and it's a sad sight. First he peers around, squinting and poking his chin forward this way and that. Then, when he finally sees it, it takes him a good ten minutes of shuffling to go get it.

So, for my first random act, I decided I would take the paper to their step whenever it's way off course.

I'd have started right away but it slipped my mind on Monday. Then, on Tuesday, it was raining so Dad drove me to school, which meant another day missed.

Dad loves a chance to trap me in the car. There's something about being enclosed in metal that gives him the courage to ask questions he wouldn't try to get away with anywhere else.

"I've been meaning to ask—how was last weekend at your mother's place?" he said as he shifted into reverse and started to ease the car down the driveway toward the street.

"Fine," I said.

"Did the *two* of you do anything special?"

Emphasizing the word "two" was Dad's subtle way of asking if my mom's boyfriend, Ray, was around.

"Not really," I said. "We rented a movie and went for a nature walk along Breval Creek Pass. That was about it."

"How was the movie?"

"It was okay." I knew he was hoping I'd mention the title but I kept that to myself. That was for his own good, because I knew he'd torture himself trying to figure out if it was the kind of show we'd have watched if Ray was around. (He was.) For someone whose job is to help other people solve their problems, Dad hasn't done so great adjusting to his own divorce. Not that he'd agree with me about that—he thinks he's totally handling it.

I wasn't in favour of the divorce myself, at first. Who wants to see their parents split up? But once I got used to the changes, I had to admit that things were better. Not because my folks had gone around screaming and throwing dishes at each other or anything like that when they were together, but you could feel the strain anyway. There was all this civilized hostility— little barbs you'd miss if you didn't know all the behind-the-scenes stuff, which, obviously, I did. Fake smiles and conversations that were so polite and distant they could have been strangers. I put a lot of energy into acting super-cheerful, like that might turn the happy family illusion into reality. After Mom moved out, the uncomfortable tension that had been in the air all the time disappeared. I felt as though I was relaxing in my own home for the first time in ages.

Everyone asks me why I decided to stay with my dad. Actually, *I* didn't decide anything. My parents worked it out and told *me* what was going to happen. I'd live with Dad and spend some weekends and evenings and holidays with Mom. I know it's more common for kids to spend the bigger chunk of time with their mother, and, to be honest, I was a bit puzzled—and hurt—at first, that my mother hadn't put up a fight for me. But the way they explained it all made sense. They said this would be the least disruptive to my life, and that one major change was enough for me to deal with. If I'd gone with Mom, it would have meant moving to a new house and changing schools, too. My folks thought that would be too much for me to handle, on top of the divorce. In the end, I was kind of relieved.

For the most part, it's been okay. At least, Mom and I have adjusted, and I think Dad's making progress. Except for slips, like this morning.

Luckily, it's a short drive to school, so he didn't have much time to grill me. I was out of the car the second it stopped. He told me not to forget I had to work that evening. As if I'd forget after I nearly wore out my voice box begging him to hire me. I gave him a quick wave to let him know I'd heard and hurried toward the school.

Jenna was waiting by my locker when I got there.

"I just did my first one," she whispered.

"Your first what?"

"You know," she said. She made a weird face, which, strangely enough, helped me get what she meant.

"Oh, rand——" I was silenced by her hand being clapped over my mouth. (At least she didn't feel the need to twist my arm.)

"Why don't you just announce it over the P.A.?" she asked, glaring.

I glared back until she peeled her hand off my face. "There's no one else close enough to hear," I pointed out. "Do you think the lockers might be bugged?"

"You can't be too careful," Jenna said, because she's not a big fan of admitting when she's wrong. "Anyway, like I was saying, I did my first one."

"Yeah? What was it?"

Jenna looked around like there might be ninjas lurking in the shadows. Then she leaned in close and whispered, "I brought a stack of teen magazines from home and put them in the student lounge for anyone who wants them."

"Uh, good one," I said, trying to sound enthusiastic. Somehow, I'd been expecting something just a smidge more impressive after the big cloak-and-dagger buildup.

"I'm doing something for the teachers one day this week, too," she added, blushing a little.

I was instantly suspicious. Last semester, Jenna had a mad crush on the new French teacher, Monsieur Poitras, even though he's a newlywed and mentions his wife, Marguerite, at least once a week. Jenna swears she's over the crush but I've never been totally convinced.

The first bell rang then, and since my homeroom is down about a mile of corridors I grabbed my books, told Jenna I'd see her at lunch, and hurried off.

Dad and I ate takeout Chinese food right out of the cardboard cartons when he got home from work that night. We often have takeout or something quick like omelettes and salad on work evenings, because we have to get to Therapy Solutions by 6:30.

"I hope you didn't feel I was grilling you about your mother this morning," he said, while moo goo gai pan dangled wetly from his fork.

"You're dripping sauce on your shirt," I said,

jabbing my chopsticks into the chow mein and scooping a glob into my mouth.

"This stuff is clear," he said. "It'll disappear when it dries. Did you hear what I said about this morning?"

"Yeah, I heard you. I just wish you'd stop obsessing over Mom."

"I'm not *obsessing* over your mother," he said. His fork paused in mid-air again and more sauce dripped, this time onto his sleeve. "I just like to make sure things are going well for you, on your weekends."

If I wasn't careful, this was going to lead to a Frank and Open Discussion (on the drive to work, of course). I made a noncommittal sound like "Ahhm," dipped a chicken ball into cherry sauce and bit into it.

"I don't know where you come up with these ideas," Dad said.

I stuffed the rest of the chicken ball into my mouth, raised my eyebrows and shrugged.

"You know, of course, that I'm trained to recognize that sort of thing," Dad said. "If I had any, ah, lingering feelings for your mother, I'd have dealt with them long ago. Good gravy, it's been a couple of years."

My point exactly, but I didn't say that. Instead, I said, "You're right. Sorry." Then I added, "You'd better change your shirt—the sauce is oily. It's definitely going to leave dark blotches."

He glanced down, frowned and went off to change as soon as he'd finished eating. I tossed my tablet, a novel we were reading for English class and a few other things into my backpack and went outside to wait. As soon as Dad came along and we got in the car I stuck in my earbuds and listened to music for the ten minutes it took to get to Therapy Solutions.

Four

Once we got there, and the overhead lights had buzzed to life, I made coffee while Dad went into the group therapy room and centred himself. I'm not exactly sure what that means but he does it every group night. It's my job to greet the clients and keep them in the waiting area until he signals that he's ready for the session to start. Add answering the phone and straightening up the magazines on the coffee table to that, and you've pretty much got my whole job description. Other than that, I just do my homework, read or play games on my tablet while the session is going on.

I decided to give Dennis a quick call before the clients started to arrive, but his phone went right to voicemail. Leaving messages isn't one of my strong points, so I didn't risk it. I dug out my novel and read a couple of pages before footsteps in the hallway told me the first of tonight's clients had arrived.

Dad's evening group consists of:

Karla, a klepto daycare worker who keeps trying to swipe the stapler and other things off my desk when I'm not looking. Miss Barducci warned me about her, but Karla is unbelievably fast and sneaky. Good thing the kids she takes care of are too big to stuff in a handbag.

Bill, a shy window-washer with a bigger than average head. He's usually the last to arrive and the first to leave, and he always has the look of someone who's skulking around. I used to wonder if he was hiding a dark secret, but now I just think he's embarrassed about being in therapy. And maybe about his head size.

Sonny, who can barely get three words out without stuttering. When the group does vocal warm-ups I can hear him in there, stammering. I asked my dad once if he could cure Sonny's problem, and he said therapy is intended to help the whole person, not just a single thing.

That didn't sound too hopeful to me but you never know.

Mrs. Wilmox, the oldest member of the group. Her husband died a few months ago, which is when she started coming to Therapy Solutions. You'd expect her to be sad, and maybe she is, but she doesn't seem that way. Unless smiling, humming and chattering away cheerfully are her ways of expressing grief.

Glenda, a single parent of three. More (a lot more, in fact) on her shortly. She'd been getting a little too friendly with my dad lately, in my opinion. I was keeping a close eye on her.

Chantal, a hairstylist who takes coming through our door as a cue to start crying. I swear, it's like throwing a switch. I see her sometimes walking across the parking lot, and she'll be waltzing along looking as happy as can be, but when she comes through the door—*wham!*—she's a blubbering basket case. (Oops, I'm not supposed to say things like "basket case" when I'm talking about my dad's work. Except nothing else quite fits what happens to Chantal.)

It was Glenda who came in first, as usual. I'd probably be early too if I had three kids at home.

"Hey, Zoey," she said with a big smile. A big win-Zoey-over-because-that-will-help-me-with-her-dad smile.

"Hello," I said, keeping my voice cool. "Would you care for some coffee?"

"Nah. The last thing I want is to be awake one minute longer than I have to be," she said, dropping into a chair. "I was up most of last night with Lucy. An earache. Looks like she'll need tubes, like Matty did. If I had a bit of sense I'd be home in bed right now."

"You do look really tired," I said. I tried to look sympathetic. "Maybe you *should* go back home and get some rest."

"Nah. The sitter will charge me anyway. I might as well stay." Glenda picked up a magazine and started flipping through it.

The phone rang.

"Therapy Solutions," I said in my most professional voice.

"Hey, Zoey. Are you busy with the crazies right now?"

"Bean! You know I'm not supposed to take personal calls at work. And don't call them that." I noticed that Glenda had stopped turning pages and was trying to look as if she wasn't eaves-dropping—which she absolutely *was*.

"Sorry. So, are you?"

"Am I what?"

"Busy with the cr … clients."

"As a matter of fact, I am."

"Okay, well, call me when you get a chance."

I told him I would and disconnected just as Sonny and Mrs. Wilmox arrived. He held the door for her and she skittered in, parked herself in a chair and started rummaging through a bright yellow bag she brings some nights. It usually means she's packing muffins or cookies for the group, but tonight she hauled out a Sudoku puzzle book and a pencil.

"I don't know how anyone can do those things," Glenda said, nodding at the puzzle book. "I tried one once and I ended up with crossed eyes and a headache."

"My dad is a total whiz at them," I said casually. That was, if not an actual lie, at least a huge exaggeration. He can do them, but there's almost always erasing involved.

If Glenda got the message (their lack of compatibility), she didn't show it. She's a smooth customer, that one.

The door opened again, this time revealing

Chantal. Her face was already crumbling in preparation for her Arrival Breakdown.

"Hi, Chantal," I called out cheerfully. I might as well have saved my breath. She lifted a hand in a half-wave, gulped in some air like she was trying to pull it together and then started blubbering. Sonny frowned slightly without looking at her. No one else paid much attention. We all knew that the crying would last for a couple of minutes and end as suddenly as it began, no matter what anyone said or did.

Karla and Bill were last to arrive, hurrying in about a minute apart just before 7:00. They'd barely taken seats when Dad buzzed me to send them all in.

I didn't actually have to do anything, since they'd all heard him on the speaker and were already standing and heading toward the door. By the time they opened it, Dad was there to greet them.

"Welcome," he said in his silky-calm therapist voice. "You are in a safe place. Please come in."

The six of them shuffled in, passing by a large wicker basket over which hung a sign instructing them to leave their inhibitions there. New clients typically stop there for a few seconds. Some even make motions as if they're putting something (their invisible inhibitions, I suppose) into the basket. But this group wasn't new, and no one even glanced at the basket on the way inside.

For the next thirty minutes all I heard from the next room was the murmur of muffled voices. Then the music started to signal the second half of the session, and there were sounds of them moving around. This made me think of that conniving Glenda, and I got a mental image of her doing some kind of sleazy, seductive dance for my dad's benefit.

The more I thought about it, the more convinced I was that she was in there, gyrating and flaunting herself in front of him. That's when I knew I had to do something to stop her—before I ended up living in a house full of children whose aching ears have them bawling all night long.

I needed advice—preferably from a guy! That reminded me I was supposed to call Bean back. And his opinion would be better than nothing. I picked up the desk phone, punched the numbers for his cell and gave him the lowdown.

"I don't think your dad can date a client," he told me through chewing sounds. "It's illegal or something."

That reassured me for about two seconds. "Yeah, but she could just quit therapy," I said, when I'd seen the flaw.

"True. But anyway, so what? Say they go out. What's the worst thing that could happen?"

"Well, duh! They could get married," I said crankily.

"Mmm," Bean said. I think he'd just taken a huge bite of whatever he was eating.

"I need to *do* something," I lamented. "Something to make sure she doesn't get her hooks into my father."

Bean was silent for a few seconds. Or as silent as you can be when you're sucking up the last few sips of a drink with a straw.

"Sorry," he said at last. "I've got nothing. When I called a while ago it was to get some ideas for our random acts. You remember, where we do *good* deeds, instead of *evil* ones."

I frowned. Then I smiled. There was no need to tell him so, but Bean had accidentally given me a helpful idea. For a change.

I made a quick excuse to get off the phone so I could think about the plan that was forming in my head without Bean chewing and slurping away in the background.

The solution to my problem was in making

Glenda happy. She was looking for romance and *I* was going to make sure she got it. Just not with my father.

Really, I'd be doing something *nice* for her. A sort of multi-purpose random act of kindness. I would good deed Glenda right out of the picture and keep my dad safe from her grimy clutches at the same time.

In case you're wondering, the fact that I don't have a lot of personal experience with romance doesn't mean I'm totally ignorant on the subject. I've read stacks of Sarah Dessen novels, and I've seen all the old classic love movies like *A Walk to Remember* and *The Notebook*.

There was one teensy-weensy problem, though—I didn't actually have anyone to set her up *with*. Luckily, I don't let little details like that get in my way. I decided I'd just invent someone. A secret admirer.

It was perfect. What female could resist that kind of mystery and romance? It would add thrills and excitement to Glenda's life, and, most importantly, it would distract her from thoughts of snagging my dad. I got to work on it right away.

By the time the clients started wandering out, I'd composed a super-intriguing note, folded it as small as possible and tucked it into her jacket pocket. It said:

*I've been watching you, and the more I see
the more I like. You don't know me (yet) but
I will get up the nerve to speak to you soon.
When I do, I think you will agree that we are
meant for each other.*

—*A Secret Admirer*

As usual, Glenda was the last to come out of the therapy room. Most weeks she finds some excuse to linger, which gives her a few minutes alone with my dad. A person would have to be blind not to see what she's up to. When she finally emerged, she came to my desk instead of leaving right away.

"Hey, Zoey," she said, "I was wondering if you might be interested in doing a little babysitting."

"Um, no, sorry," I said. Then, in my second flash of brilliance that evening, I added, "I don't really like children. I probably get that from my dad."

"Your dad doesn't like children?" she asked, looking startled.

"Goodness, no! Not even a little bit," I said. Then I lowered my voice to a whisper and added, "Of course, that's not something he goes around telling people. Don't mention it to anyone, okay?"

"Right, sure." She forced a smile, grabbed her jacket and headed for the door. I'd have loved to have taken a picture of the stunned look on her face, but Dad would never let me bring my phone to work again if I started snapping shots of the clients.

For a second or two I felt a tad guilty about the lie. Fortunately for my conscience, I decided that the random act I'd just done for her cancelled it out.

Five

My phone rang the next morning while I was searching through piles of clothes for my favourite red sweater. Half dressed, I grabbed a pillow off the bed and clutched it in front of me as I ran down the hall, listening frantically for where the ringing was coming from.

A few thrown cushions later, I found it on the floor under the end table in the corner of the living room. I vaguely remembered noticing it slide off the arm of my chair the night before, and thinking that I should get up and get it, but that's apparently as far as it went.

I swiped it on and answered. The number on the screen was unfamiliar and the name showed as "Unknown."

"Hello?"

"Zoey?" The voice was a hoarse-sounding whisper.

"Yeah?"

"I just wanted to tell you to have a great day." Same whisper, but now it sounded familiar.

"Is that you, Bean?"

Silence. I started walking backward out of the room, keeping the pillow firmly in place.

"Is *this* supposed to be your random act or something?" I demanded. "Because I was looking for my sweater and then I had to stop and run all over the house half dressed trying to find the phone."

"Why do you think I'm Bean?" Same ridiculous whisper.

"Oh, I dunno, maybe because you *are* Bean. And anyway, I don't think we're supposed to be random acting *each other*."

"Well, I couldn't think of anything to do," Bean said in his normal voice.

"So you decided to call me and whisper like a weirdo? Thanks. But just so you know, this doesn't count."

Bean sighed and made a lame excuse about guys not being good at this do-gooder slop. I broke in and told him I really had to go.

I stuck the phone into my jeans pocket and went back to my room to resume the sweater search. That's when I remembered spilling pumpkin soup on it the last time I was at Mom's. She'd kept it to launder it. I hauled on a striped top and rushed to the kitchen to grab my lunch money off the table. It wasn't there.

What a great time for Dad to forget! By then, I knew I'd be lucky to get to school by the second bell so there wasn't even time to make a sandwich. I snagged a granola bar out of the cupboard and shoved it into my backpack, which I slung over one shoulder as I headed out.

There wasn't time to stop and take the Kimuras' paper right up to their veranda but I was determined to do my random act, so I grabbed the paper from the lawn and tossed it toward the step. It would have made it, too, if it hadn't hit the railing and bounced back, sliding down between the veranda and a cedar bush. As I hurried on, I told myself that at least it was closer to their house.

I could hear the second bell ringing as I crossed the yard to the school. Late—and I still had to stop at my locker. Add a few more minutes for me to get to my classroom and there was no way I was going to make it. I'd have to go to the office for a late slip. Terrific. And it was all Bean's fault because of that stupid phone call he'd made!

I was reminded of what he'd done again at noon, in the cafeteria unwrapping my granola bar while the smell of hot dogs and fried onions on the grill taunted me.

"What's this, some kind of diet?" Jenna asked, nodding at my pathetic excuse for a lunch. It looked like a chunk of extra-dry sawdust.

"Yeah, it's called the I-didn't-have-time-to-make-my-lunch-because-I-was-on-the-phone-for-no-good-reason diet," I said. I looked pointedly at Bean.

Bean glanced up from the plastic dish in front of him. Specifically, the dish that was loaded with penne pasta in a rich sauce with big fat meatballs, red peppers and hunks of sausage.

"Why, who called?" Jenna asked.

"*Bean* called," I said. I stared at the overloaded fork that was on its way to his mouth. "He called to wish me a nice day."

"Really? Why?" Jenna looked back and forth between us, like she was trying to but couldn't quite grasp the joke.

"He thought he could pass it off as one of his random acts," I whispered, imitating how he'd sounded.

"You have no actual proof it was me," Bean said through a mouthful of food.

"It was your voice," I pointed out.

"But was it my number?" he asked smugly.

"No, it wasn't. That was really clever," I said. "So, whose phone were you using?"

"My sister's!" The triumph in his voice faded as he realized he'd accidentally confessed. Not that there'd been any doubt of his guilt. Bean shrugged, smirked and jabbed his fork back into the pasta. I watched as he drove another small shovelful into his mouth, wondering when he was finding time to chew and swallow the humungous bites he kept shoving in.

"So, because of *Bean*, I was late and only had time to grab this," I said, nodding sadly toward my granola bar. It was looking even less appealing. I stared at his pasta again and said, "*His* lunch looks awfully good, though."

The desperate longing in my eyes finally penetrated Bean's brain. His arms snaked around his food and his eyes narrowed.

"Why don't you just buy something?" Jenna asked.

"My dad forgot to leave me lunch money."

"So! It's really your father's fault!" Bean said.

"It's really *your* fault," I said. "So give me a meatball right now!" I wondered why I'd wasted my time waiting for him to offer.

He stabbed one with his fork and passed it over. I ignored the mournful look on his face and stuffed the whole thing into my mouth. It was hot and spicy, coated with marinara sauce and absolutely delicious!

A commotion had started up in another part of the cafeteria, but my brain was totally committed to the meatball, so I missed the first part of it. It wasn't until Destiny Desotto ran past our table that I started to pay attention. Her eyes were crazy-wild and she had her hand over her mouth, which didn't quite block the wails that were coming out of her.

"What's *that* about?" Jenna asked.

"She seems upset," I said.

"Wow! You could have a future as a detective," Bean said.

"And you could have a future as a starving comedian," I shot back.

"Ow, my side," he said. One of his standby lines. He used to go into a mini routine about how we'd made him laugh so much it hurt (all delivered in a sarcastic deadpan, of course) but now we mostly get the condensed version.

I ignored it, gnawed off a dry piece of my granola bar and gave him a menacing look.

"It's probably nothing," Jenna commented, still watching the sideshow. "You know how much of a drama queen Destiny is."

Now *that* was an understatement. If there's

one thing Destiny knows how to do, it's create drama. But fleeing the room seemed odd. What kind of self-respecting drama queen would leave behind a ready-made audience like a cafeteria full of people? Not to mention the fact that her friends would have to hunt her down before they could declare their everlasting loathing for whoever had caused her distress.

Sure enough, a dozen or so girls rushed out of the lunchroom, shoulders and faces thrust forward, as if a drama magnet was drawing them along. At the same time, a buzz of questions swelled among those of us who didn't much care that she was upset but wouldn't mind knowing what had set her off.

"There they go," Bean snorted. "It's like that scene in *The Wizard of Oz* where the flying monkeys hurry off to defend the wicked witch."

The commotion died down within a couple of minutes, but it wasn't long before I discovered what it had been about. I was headed back toward the cafeteria after a quick trip to the girls' washroom when I heard my name and turned to see Dennis Fuller behind me.

"Hey," he said. "Did you decide yet? About Lend a Hand?"

"I guess I can do it," I said, disappointed that I'd lost my reason to call him.

"Great!" he said. "And a few new members might cheer Destiny up after what happened earlier."

"Right. What was that all about, anyway?"

"You haven't seen it yet? Check your phone—someone will have forwarded it to you by now, guaranteed. It's all over the school."

Sure enough, when I switched my phone on, it was there—from four different senders. I couldn't read it at first but it was obviously a photo of a magazine quiz. I enlarged the top part and felt the blood drain from my face.

The heading to the quiz was "Beauty Inside and Out: How I See Myself." Underneath that, Destiny's name was written in cursive, and as I scrolled down through the questions, answers appeared in the same loopy handwriting. Specifically, *my* handwriting.

It took less than a second to realize that this page was out of one of the magazines Jenna had donated to the student lounge as her first random act of kindness. Brother.

My brain darted back to the day we'd done the quiz. The three of us, hanging out, bored. Jenna, flipping magazine pages, pausing at the quiz, reading the heading. Bean making a snickering remark about how Destiny would fill it in.

The rest of the memory is a bit blurred. I'd

grabbed the magazine from Jenna and jotted down "Destiny's" answers, which got more and more outrageous as we made our way through the questions. The worst thing was a sketch at the bottom—Destiny with exaggerated proportions, and arrows pointing to body parts that were described as "perkiest ever" and "scrump-de-bumpalicous."

For the record, we honestly hadn't meant any harm. It was just one of those situations where a few friends are messing around. The quiz wasn't something Destiny was ever supposed to see.

Now, thanks to Jenna's random act, it was everywhere. In *my* handwriting. It was going to be hard to explain if anyone recognized that the writing was mine. There's not a whole lot of it floating around, but that didn't make me feel safe. A single page in the wrong hands—a note, a bit of schoolwork—and I was sunk.

"You okay?" Dennis asked, interrupting my panicked thoughts.

"Yeah, sure. Of course I'm okay," I practically shrieked. "Why wouldn't I be?"

Dennis looked startled and took a step backward, because that's the way a normal person reacts to someone turning into a lunatic right before their eyes. I tried to recover with a light laugh but it came out a tad maniacal.

Dennis was still staring when I mumbled I'd see him later and bolted.

Bean and Jenna both had their phones out when I got back to the cafeteria. Their horror-stricken faces told me they'd been sent the quiz too. I slid into my seat and leaned forward.

"Look at the mess you got me into," I hissed at Jenna.

"I'm *so* sorry," she said. "I completely forgot about that."

"Sorry won't help if I get busted," I said, keeping my voice at a whisper.

Suddenly, Bean burst out laughing.

"I'm glad you find it funny," I muttered. But a glance at him told me Bean wasn't laughing at my predicament. He was laughing at some of the things we'd written on the quiz.

Jenna shook her head in disbelief as Bean chuckled again. She reached across the table, put her hand on my arm and said, "It'll be okay. Lots of people have similar writing. No one will know."

I could only hope she was right.

Six

I can't say I slept well that night, so I was a little bedraggled when I got to school on Thursday. The morning started out with Jenna dragging me, half awake, to the girls' washroom. I hadn't even had a chance to go to my locker.

"What's going on?" I asked.

It seemed like a perfectly reasonable question, but Jenna frowned and shushed me. Then she walked along the row of toilet stalls, bending over and peeking to make sure they were all empty.

"Okay, listen up. I have a plan and I need your help," she whispered, once she was satisfied we were alone.

"I don't think you need to whisper," I said, "since you already made sure no one else is in here."

She ignored that, and continued in her under-cover Random Act club voice. "I brought cookies for the teachers' lounge, but the only time I can take them in without anyone seeing me is when the teachers are all in class."

"You don't need me for that," I pointed out.

"I *do* need you—as a lookout. If a teacher comes along, you can signal to warn me as soon as they open the door. Just say something to them—make it good and loud, so I can hear you—and I'll hide in the staff bathroom until they leave."

"What if they're going in there to *use* the bathroom?"

"They won't be able to because I'll be in it, with the door locked."

"So, they'll just wait."

"They can't wait too long. They'll have to get back to class. I figure they'll give up and use the student bathroom instead. Once they're gone, you can open the door and let me know the coast is clear."

I can't say I was keen to do it, especially after the magazine fiasco, but Jenna can be relentless. I knew if I argued with her I'd make myself late for class, and I'd probably end up doing what she wanted anyway. So I gave in. We decided on a time for our operation, and then

I synchronized my watch with Jenna's and went off to homeroom.

And then? Okay, so I got distracted. Is that a crime? It's hard not to get caught up in the things going on around you. Like Abhati doing her best to act like she didn't notice Zach's big, brown, lovesick eyes on her. Or Julian shuffling through his books as if he was looking for an assignment that everyone knew he probably hadn't done in the first place.

Luckily, someone a few seats behind me must have missed breakfast. The sound of a stomach rumbling made me think of food, which reminded me of the cookies.

I looked at my watch. Uh-oh. Seven minutes late. I stuck my hand up, asked to be excused and speed-walked down the hall. You don't run in our school if you want to get somewhere quickly. It's a sure way to get stopped and lectured and given a noon-hour detention.

Jenna didn't look too happy when I got to the door to the teachers' lounge. What she did look was ridiculous, since she'd stuffed the cookie container under her hoodie. I didn't think the big, square bulge was going to throw too many people off the fact that she was trying to hide something.

"You're late!" she whispered.

"So? Then go do it already," I said. "Does this really seem like the best time to lecture me about tardiness?"

She glared, looked up and down the hall and darted into the room. And, naturally, the second she was inside, a teacher came around the corner. Not just any teacher, either. It was Mr. Dugas, who's the last person you want to see if you have something to hide. He has a naturally suspicious nature—the kind of teacher who thinks students are constantly pulling stuff behind his back. Which they *are*, actually, but only because they know he's so paranoid.

If anyone was going to realize that something was up, it was Dugas.

Even worse, I suddenly realized that Jenna's plan was flawed. There was no way she could hide in time. The second he opened the door he was going to see her in the room. I had to think fast, or Dugas was going to catch her in there— or see her coming out.

By then he was only a couple of steps away from where I was standing, which was no more than a few feet from the door. I moved quickly, hurrying past him, at which point I yelped and threw myself on the floor.

"Ow! Ow, ow!" I cried. Luckily, the pain

from my elbow slamming onto the floor when I landed helped me sound convincing.

Mr. Dugas did an about-face and hurried to my side.

"What happened?" he asked, leaning over me.

I moaned and rolled around a bit. Behind him, the door to the teachers' lounge opened and Jenna peeked out. I jerked my head to signal her to get out quickly, and flailed my arms and legs at the same time to make it look like it was all one big spasm.

Jenna slipped into the hallway and then stood there staring at me. Meanwhile, Mr. Dugas was asking questions, like should he go get help or did I think I could stand if he helped me up or what.

"No, no, I think it's easing up," I groaned.

"What is?" he asked.

"Leg cramp," I said through clenched teeth. "Really bad one."

He frowned. "It just came out of nowhere?"

I sat up and rubbed at my leg. "I guess."

Jenna had gotten her brain under control enough to move again, and she walked up to me as though she'd just come down the hall from that direction.

Dugas glanced at her but he turned back to me right away. There was a frown starting up on his face. "Very peculiar," he said, looking more skeptical by the second.

"Oh, no! Did you have one of your seizures, Zoey?" Jenna asked. I want to give her the benefit of the doubt, so I'm assuming she meant to be helpful.

"You have seizures?" Dugas asked.

"Well, um, not the regular kind," I said. I had the feeling that I was sinking fast and there was no way to save myself.

"She has a really rare condition," Jenna said, being helpful again. "There are only four people in the whole world with it."

"Really? And what is this condition called?" Dugas asked.

"Groponimitis," I mumbled. "It's not in most medical books yet."

Dugas looked back and forth between Jenna and me. He crossed his arms over his chest. He took a deep breath, which puffed out his cheeks as he slowly let it out.

"All right, Zoey, on your feet. Now, what are you girls up to?"

I moved as slowly as I could, trying to buy time to think. It didn't help.

"We were cutting class," Jenna blurted. She hung her head in shame, which might have been a bit more convincing if she hadn't peeked up to see if he was buying it.

He wasn't.

"Is that supposed to explain Miss Dalton's little performance on the hallway floor?" he asked.

"No, sir," I said. "I don't know what came over me. I just panicked."

Dugas stared at me.

"I'm very sorry," I added. That part was true. I was sorry I'd ever let Jenna drag me into her lamebrained scheme.

Well, the end result was that we both got three noon-hour detentions, and a letter to take home to our parents. I decided to save mine for my mom to sign when I was at her place on the weekend. My parents both claim to believe that if I get a consequence for something at school they don't need to add to it, but there's a difference in practice. Mom would sign the letter, tell me school's important and I shouldn't pull stuff like that and forget it. Dad, on the other hand, would sign the letter and immediately start probing for signs of deeper, underlying problems. *That* I could live without.

Noon-hour detentions suck. Especially three of them. I hoped the teachers enjoyed their stupid cookies.

I was trying to decide whether or not Jenna had apologized enough (three Post-it Notes, seven texts and two voicemails) to be let off the hook when Glenda came waltzing in to Therapy Solutions that evening. She was even earlier than usual, and she plunked herself into the chair closest to my desk.

"How's it going?" she asked, giving me a big, bright smile.

"Fine," I said. I noticed her top was a little tighter than it needed to be. Not the best sign that the note I'd planted in her jacket had done its job.

"School today?" Glenda said.

"Yes," I said pointedly. "We always have school on Thursdays." I suppose that might have been a bit rude, but then it wouldn't hurt for her to realize what any future stepmom of mine would be in for.

Glenda looked a bit startled, but she blinked it off and managed to smile again. "I used to think school was a drag," she said. "The only thing that made it bearable some days was seeing my boyfriend. We were in the same grade."

I couldn't help wondering where she was

going with this sudden desire to chit-chat. Then I had one of my brilliant bursts of inspiration.

"My boyfriend isn't in school," I told her.

"Oh?"

"Nope. He's a musician," I explained.

"So he's in a band?"

"Not yet, but when he gets a guitar, he's going to start one. He also collects car parts. He's actually building a whole car from pieces."

"How *old* is your boyfriend?"

"Nineteen. Guys my age are *so* immature."

"*Nineteen*," Glenda repeated weakly.

"His name is Nick," I said in my cheeriest voice. "Only everyone calls him Sloth. It's so cute. Sometimes he channels Tupac's spirit."

"Has your father met, uh, Nick?" Glenda asked.

"Sure," I said. "Dad likes him better than the last guy I went out with. He was kind of a loser."

"Well," Glenda said, which was when she seemed to run out of words. She blinked and cleared her throat. Her eyes dropped to her lap and I swear they were glistening like she was about to cry. I thought I might explode from the effort of keeping a straight face. It was great.

Why hadn't I realized sooner that *this* was the best way to discourage her from trying to get her hooks into my dad? Who would want a guy with a messed-up teenager attached?

"Hey!" I said, which made Glenda's head snap back up. "I just had a great idea. If you still need a babysitter, maybe *Nick* could watch your kids for you."

It was hard not to laugh at the way her eyes bulged at that suggestion. She stammered and stuttered and eventually managed to tell me thanks but no thanks.

I figured that should get rid of any idea she had about dating my dad. Even so, I decided to go ahead with another note from her anonymous admirer, as a bit of extra insurance. I wrote it as soon as the group went in. Or actually, as soon as I found a spare pen—the one on the desk had disappeared (not surprisingly) just as Karla passed by. Anyway, this note was even better than the first one. It said:

> I think about you all the time. Every moment
> that goes by I like you more and more. One
> of these days you will turn around and I will
> be there. I know we are meant to be together.
> Until we meet face to face, I will always be
> YOUR Secret Admirer.

The only thing left to figure out was what to do with it. It would probably make her suspicious if she found another note in her jacket pocket right after her therapy session. She might even think it was from one of the other group members, which would be bad. If I was counting my notes as good deeds (which, clearly, they *were*, seeing as how they'd help build her confidence), it was important that she could fantasize that they were from someone cool and exciting—not someone in therapy with her.

The obvious solution didn't hit me until group was almost over, which made executing it more than a little risky. Heart pounding, I hurried to the main floor and dashed out to the parking lot. I'd seen Glenda drive up in a red car with a dent in the back fender so I knew which one was hers. It was parked near the middle of the row, looking a bit pathetic next to the newer vehicles. I slipped the note under the windshield wiper, then sprinted back to the building and up the stairs as fast as I could.

Even so, I barely made it to my desk before Bill's giant head poked into the room. The group came trailing out behind him, and if anyone wondered why I was flushed and gasping for breath, they didn't ask.

For once, Glenda wasn't the last one to leave. Another sign that my plan was working. She gave me an oddly sad smile and a little wave as she was leaving.

All in all, I decided the evening was a success.

Seven

Passing the Kimuras' place on Friday morning, I caught sight of the newspaper on the lawn, which reminded me that I hadn't been exactly consistent about that particular random act. I walked over and leaned down to pick it up, feeling good about doing something kind for these feeble old folks. I wasn't late for school, so there was no rush, and I was about to take it over and put it on the veranda when I heard a shout.

"Hey! You!"

Looking up, I saw Mr. Kimura, dressed in saggy pyjamas, making his way down the steps. He took one step at a time, in three stages. First, his cane came down with a little thud, then his left foot and finally his right. A little shuffle forward brought him to the edge of each step, where the whole process was repeated.

The sight of his slow progress reminded me of the effort I was saving him, and my heart swelled with pride. I smiled and started toward him.

Oddly, he met my smile with an angry frown, and as he reached the ground he lifted the cane and thrust it out toward me.

"Very bad girl!" he proclaimed, shaking the cane in the air like some mad conductor. "Very bad!"

"Uh, Mr. Kimura," I said, perplexed by his strangely ungrateful attitude, "I think you might have the wrong idea."

"*I* not have wrong idea," he said. "*You* have wrong idea—steal paper!"

"Oh, no," I said quickly. "I'm not *stealing* the paper, I was—"

"You steal paper on Wednesday also!" he cried, cutting me off.

"I did not!" I said. I meant to sound indignant, but it came off as loud and a little rude.

"Yes, you steal," he said, nodding vigorously. "Wednesday. My wife see you pick up paper … and when I look—is gone!"

"Oh, I see." I forced a smile back onto my face. I remembered how I'd been in a hurry that day, and had accidentally sent their paper flying between a bush and the veranda. "You think I took the paper, but I didn't."

"Oh, no? So, where *is* paper?" he demanded.

"I threw it behind the bush," I explained.

We were face to face by then. Mr. Kimura snatched Friday's paper from my hands.

"You throw behind bush?" he repeated, like every one of those words was new to him.

"Yes, over there." I pointed to the bush in question. "But it was an accident."

"*How* accident? Something make you come in yard and throw paper?" He didn't seem in the least pacified at the thought that I hadn't stolen his paper after all.

I tried to tell him that I'd been trying to do something nice for them, only I'd kind of botched it because I'd been rushing for school. Unfortunately, every attempt I made to explain turned into a jumble of nonsense.

"You! Stay off yard!" he shouted, cutting off my final attempt to clear it up.

"But, I—"

"I call police!" he cried. "Press charges!"

It seemed hopeless. I mumbled that I was sorry and left, red-faced with frustration and embarrassment. Behind me, I could hear him announcing to no one in particular that I was a very bad girl. Very bad.

The newspaper episode didn't exactly put me in the mood to listen to Jenna's scheme-of-the-day when I got to school. This one was a reverse of the cookie fiasco. She wanted me to help her get her container back from the teachers' lounge.

"My mom will freak if she notices it's gone," she said. "She's kind of weird about her Tupperware."

"Why didn't you just put the cookies in a plastic bag in the first place?" I grumbled.

"What's the good of asking me that now?" she said. "It's not like I can go back and do it over."

"Do *what* over?"

We turned to find Bean standing there. Jenna's face lit up the way it does when she has an idea.

"Say, Bean, could you do me a little favour?"

He took a step back. "Like what?"

She looked him over as if she was thinking. Then she said, "Never mind, you'll chicken out and I'll have to do it myself anyway."

Of course, after that, Bean insisted on going in there after the cookie container, and Jenna let him "persuade" her into trusting him with the task.

He got it without a hitch. Walked in there and picked it up halfway through the afternoon. And then, after going on about how her mom would react if she didn't get it back right away, Jenna stuck it in her locker.

"I have too much stuff to lug home as it is," she said. "And I can't carry it out in the open— it'll give me away."

"True," Bean said. "I wonder if that might be because you have it covered with labels."

"Two labels, Bean. That's not exactly covered. I had to put 'Help Yourself' on it. Otherwise, no one would have known they were there for everyone. And I had to list the ingredients in case of allergies."

"Ignore him," I said. "He's just trying to be annoying."

"Like he has to try." Jenna clicked her locker shut and turned back to us. "Are you guys doing anything tomorrow?"

"I'm never doing anything," Bean said, "which is my chief goal in life."

"I'm at my mom's this weekend," I said. "Why?"

"I need a reason to get out of going to the nursing home with my folks," she said with a sigh.

"To see your great-uncle?" Bean asked. "The one who doesn't recognize anyone?"

"Right. Honestly, I don't understand what the point is. He doesn't even seem to know we're there. Four hours total in the car, and for nothing, really."

"Maybe he knows on some level," I said.

Jenna shrugged, as if it didn't matter to her either way. I knew better. She puts on a tough act sometimes, but she's a softie inside.

"Maybe you can do a random act while you're there," I said.

She perked up a little at that, and I could see that ideas were already stirring.

I headed home then, since Mom would be along to pick me up soon and my stuff wasn't packed for the weekend. It was a relief to see that Dad's car wasn't in the driveway yet. He's home early a lot of the Fridays when I go with Mom.

I was shoving clothes into my tote when I heard Mom beep her horn to let me know she was there. I grabbed my phone and purse, tossed the tote's strap over my shoulder and hurried out to the car. Dad was just pulling in.

"I thought you gals would be gone by now," he said, nearly falling over himself as he jumped out of his car.

Mom gave him a little wave as I slid into the passenger seat and clicked my seatbelt on. She told him to have a good weekend and he said the same to her as she eased the car out onto the street.

I got a lump in my throat when I glanced back and saw him standing there, watching us drive off. It was almost enough to make me feel guilty about scaring Glenda off. Almost.

I'd never wondered before if my father might be lonely, and the thought bothered me. He had a few friends he hung out with once in a while. They played chess, watched Coen brothers movies, went to poetry readings—that sort of thing. Except, I knew it wasn't the same as having someone special in your life.

Not that he'd never dated since he and Mom split up. There were a couple of women he took out a few times, but I never met them, so they obviously weren't very important to him.

Maybe it was time he had someone in his life, I thought. (Someone without a house full of little kids, of course.) I was thinking that over when I realized Mom was talking to me.

"I asked what you'd prefer for dinner."

"Oh, sorry. I was thinking about Dad. What are the options?"

"The salad bar at Green's, or sushi. Is something bothering you, about your father?"

"Salad bar. And it's just that I've been wondering if Dad might be, you know, a bit lonely."

Mom gave me a sideways glance. She looked

as though she was giving it some serious thought, but when she spoke, all she said was, "Salad bar it is."

The salad bar turned out to be the high point of the weekend. We went shopping for a new sports bra for me on Saturday and watched a movie on the PVR in the evening. Ray wasn't around at all. Mom said he was helping a friend move to a town a few hours away.

"Do you ever wish you were still with Dad?" I asked while Mom was fast-forwarding through commercials. I think the question surprised both of us. She pressed pause.

"No, but sometimes I wish I still *wanted* to be with him," she said.

Maybe it was the same for my father. Maybe he wasn't wishing he had my mom back so much as wishing things had turned out differently for them.

That thought made me sad, and I hadn't quite shaken off the feeling a bit later when the movie was over. Mom was reading and I was on my tablet when a message from Dennis lifted my mood. He wanted to know if I could make it to an emergency meeting on Sunday.

"Would it be okay if I went out for a while tomorrow afternoon?" I asked Mom. Since I only spend four full days a month at her house, I don't usually plan anything else when I'm with her.

"Something special going on?" Mom asked.

"More like some*one*," I said.

Mom put down her e-reader and shifted on the couch to face me.

"His name is Dennis," I went on. "He's really nice."

"And what were you two planning?"

"It's not just the two of us," I said quickly. One of my parents' strictest rules is no one-on-one dating until I'm older, and though this wasn't actually a date, I didn't need more trouble. I told her a bit about Lend a Hand, ending with a detail I should probably have kept to myself—that I'd really only joined because of Dennis.

"Sounds awful—helping people out that way," Mom said. "It's lucky there's a boy to give you a *good* reason to be part of it."

I was tempted to tell her about the random acts that Bean and Jenna and I were doing, but we'd sworn to keep it a secret, and a promise among friends isn't something to be taken lightly. So, I laughed off her sarcasm and texted Dennis that I'd be there.

Eight

The Lend a Hand meeting was at Viola Flockart's place. She lives in a sprawling house at the bottom of a cul-de-sac, and when Mom dropped me off there I could see a group gathered in the yard. Maybe Viola had decided to hold the meeting outside because it was an unusually warm day for October. Or maybe her mother took one look at the hordes of kids arriving and locked the doors. Not a lot of parents would be thrilled to have what must have been around forty kids in their house at once.

As I got close I noticed Dennis was already there—surrounded by a cluster of girls. As usual. Well, they could make fools of themselves if they liked. I wasn't about to join them.

I walked past the others and wandered over to a table where cold drinks had been set out in tubs of ice. As I helped myself to a bottle of lemonade, I snuck a look at a guy who was relaxing on a deck chair nearby. I might not have had much experience at this stuff, but I'd read all the right magazines so I knew the best way to get Dennis's attention would be to act interested in someone else. This was a perfect opportunity.

I took a couple of steps toward the deck chair guy, but he didn't even seem aware I was there. That was when I realized his attention was focused on his phone, which was occupying both his eyes and his thumbs.

"It sure is hot," I said.

Nothing.

I cleared my throat and repeated it a bit louder, which was enough to get him to drag his attention away from the screen long enough to glance at me. When he did, he raised both eyebrows, like he couldn't quite believe someone was interrupting his Angry Birds game, or whatever it was that had him so engrossed. He looked sort of familiar but I couldn't quite place him. Probably a student from the high school, which is right next door to Breval Middle School.

"This is my first time," I said, flashing him a big smile. "At a Lend a Hand meeting, I mean."

"Fascinating," he said.

Clearly, this guy wasn't part of the Lend a

Hand crowd. Even clearer was the fact that he wasn't in the mood for a friendly chat. I got that. It was time to walk away, and I would have done just that if I hadn't glanced toward the others and found Dennis looking straight at me.

I turned back to deck chair guy, nodded and laughed as if he'd just said something hilarious. His eyebrows, which seemed to be his main method of communicating, rose even higher than they had before.

"Uh, I'm Zoey," I said, as if he'd just asked me my name. I made myself smile again but, judging by the way he shifted in his chair, it might have come out looking a bit demented. Or maybe there was some other reason he seemed to be positioning himself to leap to his feet and make a run for it. Either way, I could *not* let Dennis see that happen.

"Look," I said, "I know you probably think I'm a nut-job or something, but I can explain."

He looked skeptical, to say the least.

"There's a guy over there who I kind of like," I said.

"The one heading this way?" he asked before I could get any further.

I darted a look and saw that Dennis had indeed broken free from the circle of girls and was coming toward us.

"That's *him*," I hissed to deck chair guy. "Look, could you *please* play along? All I'm asking is that you flirt a teensy bit."

I didn't get any promises, but deck chair guy suddenly seemed to be in much better spirits. Probably it was the relief of knowing that he wasn't facing down a deranged person after all. Or maybe he was simply amused. I didn't care which it was, as long as he wasn't scowling and cringing.

Dennis had crossed the space between us by then. He paused at the table and grabbed a root beer, screwed off the top and tipped it up. I watched his Adam's apple bob as he glugged down a third of the bottle before lowering it and looking at me.

"We're going to start in a minute," he said.

"Okay."

"Do you *have* to go, Zoey?" deck chair guy asked. He leaned forward and gave me a sad, imploring gaze. I was pleased that he was co-operating, but the acting was a bit over the top.

"Yeah, sorry," I said. To my delight, Dennis shot the guy a look of clear disgust. Yes!!

That's where it ended because Amanda Trecartin chose that exact second to bang a pair of ice tongs on a metal umbrella pole and yell, "Okay, people, let's get this meeting started."

Dennis and I joined the others in a semicircle facing Amanda.

"Where's Destiny?" someone asked.

"Destiny won't be here today," Amanda said. "I'll explain why in a minute, but for today I'll be running the meeting."

"Who's taking notes?" a thin girl near the front asked. "Destiny said we're supposed to keep track of everything we do."

"I *know* that," Amanda answered. She sounded testy, but she pulled herself together and tried to look pleasant as she scanned the group in front of her.

"Any volunteers?" she asked.

Dennis glanced my way, like he was wondering if I was the kind of person who would step up— someone who could be counted on. I decided I was, and the next thing I knew a notebook had been thrust into my hands and I was jotting down useless information. Call to order, attendance, blah, blah, blah. It all seemed a bit ridiculous to me but I kept that opinion to myself.

I was barely paying attention to the nonsense I was writing because my mind had drifted off to a more romantic setting—one where Dennis and I were alone and he was about to tell me how long he'd been trying to find the courage to ask me out. His eyes were full of devotion and I was tipping my face up toward him when Amanda's awful words came crashing into my fantasy.

"I'm sure you've all heard about the vicious attack on Destiny. She can't even be with us today because of the pain it caused her. Now she needs us, and we're going to *lend her a hand*."

An uneasy feeling stirred in my stomach. Surely she didn't mean …

"The person who wrote those nasty things in the magazine *must* be found!"

I could hardly believe what I was hearing. The emergency meeting I was at—and taking notes for—was about that stupid quiz. Even worse, Amanda held up photocopies of the offending page, and said, "Our best shot at exposing this person is through their handwriting. So, I want you all to take a copy of this and keep your eyes peeled for anything that might have been written by the same person."

While everyone else's eyes were turned to the stack of pages in Amanda's hands, mine dropped to the notebook I was holding. The one with handwriting identical to the samples she was about to hand out.

The first idea my brain comes up with in a crisis is generally useless. This was no exception. It screamed, "Run!" (like that wouldn't look slightly suspicious), but luckily my body was in a state of panic-freeze and refused to co-operate. That gave me time to form a slightly more rational plan, which I put into action at once.

I still had about a third of my bottle of lemonade so I unscrewed the cap, lifted it like I was going to take a drink and fumbled it so that it landed upside down smack dab in the middle of my page of notes.

"Oh, no!" I cried, grabbing at the bottle and sloshing more liquid over the paper. "I'm so sorry—the meeting notes are ruined."

"Can you still read them?" Amanda asked.

I squinted doubtfully at the page, which was perfectly legible. Why hadn't I picked root beer, like Dennis? My lemonade had barely discoloured the paper.

"I *think* I can make out what it says," I said slowly. "Tell you what—I'll take this home and dry it out, and then I'll type it up and e-mail the notes to you."

"That would be *great*," she said, as if the relief was almost too much for her.

"Okay, then," I said. I turned the soggy wad of pages upside down and waved it as if I were drying it. Of course, my real motive was to keep anyone from seeing that the handwriting was a perfect match for the writing on the page they were circulating.

It was a strange feeling when Dennis passed me a copy of the quiz. Heat that had nothing to do with the way his hand brushed mine rose in my cheeks. Everyone stopped talking and read it over, which led to some head-shaking and comments that I found just a little harsh.

Thankfully, Amanda wrapped things up quickly after that. I was about to call my mom to let her know I was ready to be picked up when deck chair guy came strolling over.

"Hey, you," he said. He was probably going for flirty, but it came out sounding a lot closer to creepy.

"Uh, hi," I said. I'd have liked to ask him what he thought he was doing, but since Dennis was still standing beside me that didn't seem wise. Instead, I willed him away with the power of my mind and what I hoped was a piercing look. Then Dennis spoke.

"We can give you a lift if you need one," he said.

"*We?*" I said.

"Me and my brother Gary," he explained, nodding to deck chair guy.

If aliens were ever planning to abduct me that would have been a good time.

Nine

It turned out that aliens weren't necessary after all. Before I could say a word, Stephanie Roth hurried over, grabbed Dennis by the arm and told him she needed to speak to him privately for a minute.

I stared straight ahead, stone-faced and determined *not* to look at Gary, a.k.a. the deck chair guy, a.k.a. Dennis's brother. And I wouldn't have, except that curiosity got the better of me when he went, "Psssst, Zoey!"

"What?" I said crossly.

"Don't worry," he said. "Your secret is safe with me."

"Yeah, right." I could picture Dennis and Gary doubled over, laughing and gasping for breath while Gary described the way I'd made a fool of myself.

"I'm serious," he told me. "I'm totally in favour of you getting your man. I think you'd be good for Dennis."

A glimmer of hope stirred in me, but I wasn't convinced. It must have showed on my face.

"You're wondering why I'd have your back when I don't even know you, right?"

I nodded.

"You're entertaining," was the unflattering answer.

"So, you'd like to have me around for sport," I said.

He laughed right out loud. "I guess, kind of," he said. "Anyway, I swear I won't say anything to Dennis about what happened earlier."

"Thank you," I said stiffly. I guess I seemed a bit ungrateful, but you can't really blame me, considering his motive for staying quiet.

"By the way," I added, "you can stop pretending to flirt with me in front of Dennis. It's not like you're good at it."

He laughed harder.

After that, I did my best to ignore him until Dennis got back. As soon as he did, he asked if I was going to take them up on the offer of a drive.

"I have to check with my mom," I said.

The absolutely strictest rule my parents have is that I never, ever, under any circumstances, get into a car with anyone unless I've cleared it with one of them first. Taking a ride with Gary and Dennis without permission would get me grounded for two weeks if I got caught.

Mom answered on the first ring. "Hey, honey!"

"Hi, Mom. I can get a drive. Is that okay?"

"With who?"

"Dennis's ... family."

I hoped she wouldn't notice the way I'd hesitated, and, for a change, luck was with me. As I ended the call, permission granted, I told myself I hadn't *really* lied. A brother was family. It wasn't my fault if she jumped to conclusions and assumed I meant his parents.

As the car pulled away from Viola's place, I was surprised to hear Dennis say, "Well, that meeting was a huge waste of time."

"What do you mean?" I said.

"Come on—*that* was the big emergency?" he said. "Ridiculous! The group should be doing things that actually help people who need it."

"Like what?" I asked, looking at him with new interest. I always thought Dennis was a nice guy but this was unbelievable. I mean, he *seriously* cared about doing good deeds.

He must have thought about it before, because he didn't hesitate before answering.

"Well, for example, there are a couple of

old people on our street. They can't take care of their yards in the summer, or shovel their walks in the winter. And they can't afford to pay anyone. Helping out someone like that would make a real difference for them. *That's* what the group is *supposed* to be about."

I agreed.

"I could care less about some silly quiz," he added.

"I wonder what they plan to do if they find out who wrote it," I said, hoping I sounded casual.

"Who knows?" Dennis said with a shrug. Of course, he had a lot less reason to be interested in the answer than I did. "But I think the idea is a bit risky."

"Risky?"

"Sure. Lots of people have similar handwriting. What if they blame the wrong person?"

"That would be terrible," I said. I meant it, too. I didn't want someone else to take the fall for this—I just didn't want to get caught myself.

We were getting close to my mom's place then, and I wasn't exactly eager to show it off. After coming from Viola's house, the thought of Dennis seeing Mom's tiny bungalow, with its scruffy yard and old clapboard siding, wasn't exactly filling me with pride. It would have been different if we'd been going to my dad's—it's not fancy, but it's a lot nicer than the place my mom bought when she moved out. You can hardly blame me for not wanting the hot guy I'd had my eye on for months to know that's where I live—even if it's just on alternate weekends.

Mom pretends to think her place has charm, and insists it's all she needs, but if anything might have made her think twice about the breakup, I bet moving into that shrunken excuse for a house would have been it. Or it could have worked the other way. Maybe seeing what she was willing to give up helped her feel sure she was making the right decision.

None of that mattered at the moment. I asked Gary to drop me off at a convenience store one block over, claiming I needed to pick up a few things. Both of them said they didn't mind waiting, but I thanked them for the drive and waved them away.

I watched their car until it was out of sight and then headed around the corner and down the street to Mom's. She was sitting out on the step. There's no veranda there, just a few cruddy cement steps that are chipped and worn. The sight of her made me instantly uneasy.

"I thought you were getting a drive home," she said.

"I did—I got dropped off at the corner so they wouldn't have to go too far out of their way."

Mom gave me a long look—the kind where I could almost swear she was reading my mind, even though I know that's impossible. I offered a feeble smile and plunked down beside her, mostly so I wouldn't have to feel her eyes on my face.

"Is Ray coming over today?" I asked, hoping distract her.

"No."

There was something in her tone that wasn't quite right, something that made me think there was more to this story than she was telling me. It was the first weekend I'd spent with her in a long time that he hadn't made a single appearance. I wanted to ask if there was anything wrong, but I wasn't sure how. And anyway, she wasn't done with me yet.

"I have to say that I'm curious about what you were hiding."

"What do you mean?" I did my best to inject innocence into my voice and it sounded sincere to me. By the look on Mom's face, that made one of us.

"I'm not stupid, Zoey. You got dropped off at the corner for a reason. It was either because you didn't want me to see who you were with, or because you're ashamed of this place. So, which is it?"

Both were sort of true—it would have spelled big trouble if my mom had caught me getting dropped off by a teenaged driver. I wasn't about to admit that, but it seemed relatively safe to cop to the other part of her theory.

"It's just not a very nice neighbourhood," I said.

"It's a poor neighbourhood. That doesn't mean it's not nice. The folks I've met around here have all been good people."

I didn't answer. Sometimes, that keeps Mom from continuing. This wasn't one of those times.

"I hope you aren't turning into someone who values people because of what they *have* instead of who they *are*," she said.

"You know I'm not like that."

"Then choose your friends wisely," she said. "Because if you pick friends who care about possessions over people, eventually you'll start to do the same."

I started to open my mouth to object, but she held up a finger and kept on.

"The two I know—Bean and Jenna—they're good kids. I'm not talking about them. I'm talking about any new friends you might happen to make."

"Dennis isn't like that, if that's who you mean."

"Glad to hear it. So, maybe next time you won't need to be dropped off at the corner."

Ten

Dennis's comments about helping people and making a real difference for them kind of inspired me, and got me thinking about the whole random acts thing. It didn't take a genius to see that it wasn't going very well. I made up my mind to step things up—look for more opportunities, put some smiles on a few faces.

That all sounds a bit vague, I suppose. That's because I hadn't figured out the details—like what I was actually going to do. But I was on high alert, a veritable random act looking for a place to happen, if you know what I mean.

This was my noble frame of mind on Monday morning when I got to my locker and found Stephanie Roth hovering nearby. She sidled up to me as I dug out the books I needed for first class.

"Hey," she said. She smiled, showing all of her teeth. Very natural looking.

"Uh, hi." I wondered what she wanted. We barely knew each other, so I found it odd that she seemed to be waiting specifically for me. Even when she'd come to talk to Dennis the day before, she hadn't as much as nodded in my direction.

"I know you left the meeting with Dennis yesterday," she said.

Aaaah. So—this was about Dennis. I switched my full attention to her, not saying anything, but waiting to see what was next. She seemed a bit on edge.

"Are you guys going out?" she blurted after a few seconds.

"He gave me a drive home," I said, carefully avoiding giving her an actual answer.

"But do you *like* him?" There was a desperate edge to her voice, and I took a step away as I swung my locker door closed.

"Sure," I said offhandedly. "Everyone likes Dennis."

She didn't buy the casual tone. Her hands went to her hips and she moved forward, closing the space between us. The extra-toothy smile had disappeared, and the only word I can think of to describe her at that moment was psycho.

(Unless you find bug-eyed and frothy-mouthed normal.)

"You *stay away from him*," she hissed. "I mean it."

"Stay away from who?" asked a voice behind me. Jenna, thank goodness. Not that she'd be much help if Stephanie went over the edge and decided to take me down right then and there, but it was a relief not to have to face this Dennis-crazed creature alone.

Stephanie threw Jenna a hostile look but she didn't say anything else before spinning on her heel and stomping away.

"Wow. What was *that* about?" Jenna asked.

"Apparently, she likes Dennis, and thinks I'm some kind of a threat to them riding off into the sunset together."

"*You?* As if!" As soon as it was out of her mouth, Jenna seemed to realize that might not have been the biggest compliment I'd ever been given. She smoothed it over by turning red and stammering something indecipherable.

I took advantage of her blunder and changed the subject before she could start to wonder where Stephanie had gotten the idea. That could only lead to a lot of questions I didn't particularly want to answer, since they'd all lead back to Lend a Hand.

"Did you get a chance to do any random acts when you visited your uncle?" I asked.

"My *great*-uncle," she corrected. "I read to a couple of the nursing home residents, but that wasn't exactly anonymous."

"It kind of was," I said. "They *saw* you, but they still didn't *know* you."

"That's true!" She seemed cheered at the thought. "So, that *would* count. I must be ahead of you and Bean."

"I didn't know we were having a competition," I said.

"Well, we're not really," she agreed. "But if we were, I'd be winning."

I didn't like the smug expression on her face. "Don't be so sure," I said. But when she turned and gave me a sharp look I grinned. "Kidding. You're probably ahead of me and Bean combined."

"Combined with what?" Bean had appeared, it seemed, out of nowhere.

When I turned to face him I felt my mouth fall open in shock. Since Friday, his appearance had undergone quite a transformation. Frosted, spiked hair had sprung up on his head, and there were two thin lines shaved in his right eyebrow. While Jenna and I gaped, Bean did his best to act like it was no big deal.

"Well, look at *you*," Jenna said.

"What? *This?*" Bean gestured vaguely toward his head, as if radical changes were an everyday happening. The truth is, he'd had the same boring hairstyle since he was in grade four.

"Wow," I said. Not "wow" as in *is this ever cool*, but more like *is this ever weird*. "So, who are you trying to impress?"

As soon as I said it, red splotches appeared on Bean's face, which was a dead giveaway. No surprise there. What else would have inspired him to turn into a middle school version of Mr. Sexypants?

"Yeah, who's the poor, uh, I mean lucky girl, Bean?" Jenna said.

"I don't know what you guys are talking about," Bean said.

"Sorry, we should have talked slower," I told him. Jenna giggled.

"Ow. My side," Bean said, with his usual straight-faced delivery.

"I think there's a mandatory retirement on lines you've used more than a million times," Jenna said. An exaggeration, but Bean does tend to overdo that one.

"And 'talk slower' is new and original?" he scoffed.

"Okay, so we could all use some fresh material," I said. "Never mind that—what happened to you this weekend?"

"Or should we say, *who* happened to you?" Jenna chimed in.

He looked back and forth at us. "Wouldn't you like to know?" he said.

"Oh, we'll know all right," I told him. "Don't even *think* you're keeping this from us."

I took a step closer to him—and his growing smirk. I leaned in a little and stared fiercely into his eyes.

"Is that supposed to intimidate me? Make me tell you everything you want to know?" Bean asked with a snicker.

"Nope," I said, grabbing his index finger and folding it back enough to encourage him to co-operate. "*This* is."

Bean's eyes popped wide open and the smile died on his face. "Hey!" he said, tugging his hand in a useless attempt to loosen my hold.

"Spit it out," I told him. And I smiled.

"Okay, okay." He hesitated for another second or two, probably thinking frantically about a way out of this one. In the end, good sense prevailed and he accepted defeat. Of course, he knew I wouldn't *really* hurt him, but he also knew I wasn't going to let go until he coughed up the details we wanted.

"Mariska Nagy," he said.

Jenna and I exchanged what were probably identical looks. A little surprise, a lot of "what the heck?" Neither of us had really gotten to know the "new girl." (And, okay, she'd lived in Breval for more than a year, but new lasts a long time in a small town.) I didn't know if she was exactly unfriendly, but Mariska mostly kept to herself. You might even have called her a bit mysterious, although that could just have been because of her exotic appearance. Large, strikingly dark eyes in a pale, triangular face gave her an almost other-worldly look.

I let go of Bean's finger. He gave me an accusing frown and tucked his hand under his leg. "It's no big deal, anyway," he said.

"I don't exactly feel like I got the whole story there, Bean," Jenna said.

"Me neither," I agreed. "Give us some details—or else."

"I ran into her at Subway on Friday night and we got talking. Then, we caught a movie on Saturday. That's it."

Jenna and I both narrowed our eyes at him menacingly.

"I guess we're kind of going out now," Bean added. "But so what? She'll probably dump me before the end of the week."

"Well, if she has any sense," I said.

It was a bit weird in an unpleasant way, thinking of Bean going out with Mariska. I know for sure I don't harbour any romantic feelings toward him, so I couldn't quite understand what *that* was about. Maybe it was the sudden change in his appearance. That was pretty jarring, although, with her unusual looks, he probably thought that would make them a more natural-looking fit.

I shrugged it off as the bell rang and we hurried off to our separate classes.

One good thing about Bean's news was that it had distracted Jenna. I could only hope it wouldn't come to her later—how she'd inter-rupted Stephanie practically threatening my life over Dennis. I wouldn't normally keep anything from Jenna—especially about a hot guy—but it would be big trouble for me if she found out about him and his brother driving me home from Viola's. She'd want to know what I'd been doing there in the first place, and there was no way I could let her or Bean find out I was having anything to do with the Lend a Hand club.

So things were getting a little complicated. So what? I told myself it was no problem. I could handle it. I'd multi-task—and find a way to do it all without being found out. How hard could it be to do Random Acts *and* Lend a Hand?

Oh, yeah. And stay out of the way of a psycho.

Eleven

I was predictably nervous about Stephanie after the Monday morning outburst, but there were no more psycho performances from her that day, and by the time school let out on Tuesday, I'd convinced myself she wasn't going to bother me again. I thought she might even be feeling embarrassed about the way she'd acted.

Since Tuesday is one of my work evenings, I did some of my homework while I was waiting for Dad to get home. He arrived with takeout for dinner: a rare treat of greasy cheeseburgers, salty fries and ice cold root beer that fizzed and tickled on its way down. We ate every bite, and headed off to Therapy Solutions.

I barely had time to put on my receptionist face before the door opened and Bill's big head stuck itself in. That was a bit of a surprise, since he'd never been the first to arrive before. I nodded and smiled and said, "Good evening," in the coolly professional way I'd perfected in front of my bedroom mirror.

Normally, I'd have been lucky if Bill gave me so much as a grunt in return, so it was a surprise when he shuffled up to the desk and cleared his throat. That seemed to suggest that words were about to follow, but Bill stood there in silence with his face getting red.

"Yes?" I said. I thought that might coax out whatever it was he wanted to say, but the sound of my voice seemed to startle him, and he leaned back so sharply I thought he might fall over. It was a wonder that he ever managed to participate in group therapy, where he had to talk in a room full of other people.

One minute stretched into two, which, with someone standing miserably in front of you, is a lot longer than you might think.

"The others will be here any minute," I said finally. I hoped that reminder would nudge him, and, sure enough, it worked.

"I want an appointment just for me," he said. He coughed slightly and then added, "Doesn't matter what day or time."

"No problem," I said. I tapped on my keyboard to open the appointment schedule and scrolled down the screen. "There's a cancellation for Thursday morning at 9:00—I can give you that slot if you like."

"Okay," he said.

"And did you want to cancel your group appointment?" I asked. When she'd trained me, Miss Barducci had explained that if a client went from group to individual therapy, or vice versa, they usually dropped out of the original sessions. But Bill shook his head.

"No," he said. "I want both."

"Okay."

I thought that was the end of it, but Bill leaned in a little, his face as serious as could be. "I need to see Dr. Dalton about something personal," he confided.

The last thing I needed was to hear something weird or gross that I'd have to carry around in my head for who knew how long. I forced myself to smile, even as I silently willed him not to say another word. It didn't work.

"The problem is," he whispered miserably, "someone is stalking me. And I don't know what to do about it."

"Someone is stalking you," I repeated, staring at him. I thought maybe he was kidding. Not that I'd ever considered Bill much of a joker.

"That's right," he said. "It's really creepy." He

glanced to his left and right, and even darted a look behind him. Maybe he thought this person was about to materialize in the room.

I was doing my best to give the guy the benefit of the doubt, but this was a hard story to swallow. When something seems doubtful, my mom likes to say that "stranger things have happened," but this was just about impossible to imagine. Bill, even if he'd had a normal-sized head, was not exactly someone you'd look at and think, hey, I bet stalkers are a big problem for this guy.

Somehow, I kept a straight face, and when I realized my mouth was hanging open I snapped it shut. Bill looked as if he might say something else, but just then the door swung open and Chantal came blubbering in, with Sonny behind her, busily sending a text message. The rule is "phones off" during therapy, which must be a strain on Sonny. That phone never leaves his hand. When he isn't sending or receiving messages, he's checking obsessively to see if he's missed any.

With the arrival of other group members, Bill clammed up and hurried to a chair, where he leaned forward and began to study the floor with his usual pre-session concentration.

Mrs. Wilmox was barely a breath behind

Sonny, yellow bag in hand. As she opened it, the smell of cinnamon flooded the waiting area.

"Guess what I have in here," she said cheerily.

The others all looked eagerly toward the bag, but I wasn't one bit interested myself. I'd decided just that morning to give up sweets for a while. Time to tone up, before my bulges became full-blown love handles.

Of course, I hadn't been expecting anyone to offer me a soft, mouth-watering cinnamon bun. With thick, creamy frosting. As Mrs. Wilmox passed them around I suddenly realized it might be rude—in fact, it would probably hurt her feelings—if I refused. So, I took the biggest one.

Glenda, who's normally early, was the last one to show up. She came in, breathless and hurrying, just as the others finished licking frosting off their fingers and filing into the therapy room.

"Kids!" she said as she scooted past my desk. I figured that was her one-word explanation for almost being late. I spent a couple of minutes wondering what kinds of bratty things they'd been doing to slow her down. It was satisfying to know I'd headed off any possibility that they'd be bringing their delinquency into my life.

I had no homework (well, none I wanted to do—I suppose I could have found some if

I'd actually looked) so I spent the next ten or fifteen minutes playing games on my tablet. I was on the verge of beating one of my own high scores when a commotion broke out in the therapy room.

I used to think there must be commotions going on in there full time, with all the strange sounds the clients made during what Dad calls the Primal Release stage of therapy. But this was different. It started with a crash, as though someone had thrown a chair or plant or something against the wall. Then there was yelling—a blend of voices: some rising, some struggling to be calm and soothing. That was followed by a bang as the door to the therapy room flew open and a wild-eyed, red-faced Karla ran out. I'd have said she was hysterical, except I'm not qualified to make an actual diagnosis.

"I am *sick* and tired of being accused of things!" she yelled, as Mrs. Wilmox and Chantal scurried out of the therapy room and took up positions at either side of her.

"Give it back," Chantal said. "You know you took it—everyone knows you took it. So stop lying and give me my pashmina."

"I don't have your stupid pashmina—and why can't you call it a scarf like everyone else?"

"I call it a pashmina because that's what it *is*,"

Chantal answered. "And don't tell me you don't have it, you lying klepto. I can see one of the fringes sticking out from under your sweater."

Karla looked down to where Chantal was pointing. Sure enough, a cluster of coral-coloured threads, knotted at the top, had worked itself into view.

"Huh!" Karla said, as though she was surprised to find it there. She reached under her sweater and tugged out the pashmina, like a magician producing one of those long, bright scarves. Then she looked at it sadly, as if she could hardly bear to part with it, and passed it to Chantal.

"That really isn't a good colour for you anyway, dear," Mrs. Wilcox said, which seemed oddly beside the point to me.

Karla shrugged. Then smiled. "I'm really sorry," she said. "I've been doing so much better lately. I don't know what happened."

"Yeah, okay," Chantal said. "I know you're working hard."

"Maybe it's time for us to let Karla know that we're here for her," came my dad's voice from the doorway.

"We're here for you, Karla," the group members said, in semi-unison.

Karla looked around, her eyes shining with gratitude. "Thanks, guys," she said. She turned to her most recent victim then and added, "Thanks, Chantal!" It was a touching moment, which ended with Karla reaching out and giving Chantal a big hug. And swiping a silver ear cuff from Chantal's left ear.

I couldn't help but find that just a little funny. Until, that is, I looked down at the desk and realized my iPhone was missing.

Twelve

Chantal retrieved her ear cuff and I got my phone back before Karla could make her escape that evening. And even though I was one of her victims, I couldn't help feeling sorry for her as she passed over the stolen items.

I don't know if I mentioned this before, but I'm not supposed to talk about my dad's clients. Ever. So, I felt a little guilty when a few details about Karla's thievery accidentally slipped out at lunchtime on Thursday. (Okay, it was the whole story—but I didn't mention any names, and I only told Jenna, so it wasn't as bad as it could have been. Besides, she swore she wouldn't tell anyone else.)

"How awful would it be if you actually couldn't stop yourself from stealing?" Jenna said. "And think of what it's like for her family and friends. They must have to watch every move she makes."

"She probably *has* no friends," I said. "Who'd want to hang out with someone who steals from them full time?"

While Jenna unwrapped her lunch, I tried to imagine what it would be like if she were a klepto like Karla. It seemed impossible any friendship could survive that.

Unaware that she was being cast in the unflattering role of compulsive thief, Jenna offered me a piece of her bagel.

"Not if it's cream cheese and strawberries." It's her favourite combination, but strawberries turn my face into red-splotch central. "They give me hives, remember?"

"I forgot, sorry. Hey, here comes loverboy."

I followed her glance to Bean and Mariska, who were just coming into view. They were headed our way, although it must have been difficult to navigate while they gazed at each other like a pair of lovesick lemurs.

"I hope their eyes don't pop out of their heads," I muttered.

"What?"

"I was just saying that they'd better watch where they're going before they trip over something."

Jenna's eyes narrowed. "Are you *jealous* of Bean?" she said.

"Don't be ridiculous." I snickered to prove I meant it, which I *did*. It was the strangest thing, how his new relationship was irritating me, but it definitely had nothing to do with any romantic interest I had in him.

"Hey, guys," Bean said as he plunked into his usual spot. After a slight hesitation, Mariska sat down beside him. She smiled at me and Jenna.

As I smiled back at her, I noticed Amanda Trecartin heading toward our table, or, I should say, toward *me*, judging by the look on her face. I'd been avoiding her since the Lend a Hand meeting, but I could see that there wasn't going to be any escape this time. Funny how I'd been nervous about Stephanie, and *she* hadn't bothered me again since the day she'd threatened me at the lockers. You know things aren't going well for you when you can't keep track of all the people you need to dodge.

"Be right back," I said, jumping to my feet and hurrying toward Amanda. I had to make sure she didn't get close enough for Bean and Jenna to hear the conversation I knew was coming.

"*Where* are the meeting notes?" Amanda asked, the second I reached her. "You said you'd send them on the weekend."

"I know. Sorry." Actually, I'd been hoping, if I avoided her for a while, she'd forget about the stupid notes and I wouldn't have to bother. Looking at Amanda's frowning face, I could see *that* plan wasn't going to work. "I've been crazy busy," I said, "but I'll get them done tonight— I promise."

"I sent you a text Sunday night," she said. "You didn't answer."

I vaguely recalled being half asleep on the couch when her nagging note lit up my phone. I'd rolled my eyes and hit delete.

"I meant to. I was just busy. How'd you get my number, anyway?"

"From Dennis."

I felt a warm glow at the thought that she'd associated me with Dennis enough to ask him for my number.

"Just make sure you send me those notes *tonight*," Amanda said then, as if she'd somehow been declared the boss of me.

I felt like telling her I'd do it when and *if* I felt like it, but it sounded like she knew Dennis pretty well and I didn't want her badmouthing me to him, so I said, "No problem," and smiled instead. She gave me a stern look and moved on.

By now, I was wondering whether all of this bother was worth it. Let's face it, I was acting on the flimsiest possible evidence that Dennis *might* have a *sliver* of interest in me. If you consider a phone call and a drive home evidence. For all I knew, he might have called dozens of people about Destiny's dumb group. But I have a stubborn streak in me, and I decided to hang in there, just in case. So, I left a reminder about the meeting notes on my phone and headed back to the table to see if my lunch was safe. Bean is not always trustworthy around unprotected edibles.

Thankfully, the food on my tray appeared to be untouched. I picked up my plastic fork and was about to dig in when I was treated to the appetite-killing sight of Mariska feeding Bean a bite of her sandwich.

A glance at Jenna told me she was just as impressed with this performance as I was. We exchanged a "how gross is this/what grade are we in anyway?" look, which didn't escape the happy couple's notice.

"Sorry," Mariska said. Her apology seemed a bit insincere, followed up as it was by giggling and eye-batting in Bean's direction.

"There are people trying to eat here," Jenna said. She forced out a fake laugh, like she was kidding, but I knew better. So did Bean. He made an effort to control himself after that, which, thankfully, encouraged Mariska to settle down too. She stopped some of the silliness and by the end of lunch had managed to say several things that bordered on sensible.

It was good to know that Jenna had also found the whole PDA thing annoying. That put an end to the worry that I might be ignoring deeply buried feelings for Bean. The simple fact was that this was a group matter. There were three of us. We *worked*. And Mariska was an intruder. She was upsetting the natural balance of things.

I decided I was going to make more of an effort to like her. Not that I'd actually disliked her up until then. I barely knew her. Like I said, her family had moved to Breval just a year ago, and she always seemed like a private type. Although going out with Bean seemed to be bringing her out of her shell.

The main thing was that if Bean was happy, then I was happy for him. It wouldn't kill me to be friendlier to Mariska. Also, I'd count it as a random act, because there's no point in wasting a perfectly legitimate good deed, now, is there?

Even after the lunchroom showdown with Amanda, I almost forgot about the meeting notes again. Dad and I were on our way to the car when my phone alert reminded me, for all the good that did. I dashed back into the house and spent a few minutes frantically tearing my room apart but I failed to turn up the lemonade-infused pages.

Just my luck. I must have left them at Mom's—and there was no way I could get Dad to stop there before session tonight. We were already running late, and Mom's house is in the opposite direction of Therapy Solutions.

I mulled over the problem on the way and decided that I could probably recreate them from memory. Not the complete attendance, but I could come up with a lot of the names and tell Amanda those were the only ones I could make out on the ruined pages. As for the meeting itself, I figured her main interest was to showcase the importance of her role. As long as I featured her and basically captured the main points of what happened, I should be okay.

I made a good start on it before the first client arrived that evening. It was Glenda, looking tired and drab. Perfect. No makeup, a plain sweater and hair tugged back into a ponytail. So much for the glamour girl who'd been trying to put the moves on my father.

Her appearance drew startled glances from Chantal and Karla as they arrived and sat down.

Chantal even dabbed away her pre-meeting tears in order to get a better look. She leaned forward.

"You okay, Glenda?"

Glenda closed her eyes and shook her head in a quick burst of movement that said she didn't want to talk about it.

Something seemed off. It was good that she wasn't glammed up, trying to entice my dad, but she wasn't acting the way you'd expect a woman with a secret admirer to act. You'd *never* have guessed there was excitement and intrigue in her life. Thanks to my random act, I knew there was, so I found that puzzling.

She stared in silence at the floor until the group went in. I couldn't help but notice that she didn't even bother saying hello to me, although she gave me a kind of mournful glance when she went by. It hadn't taken long for her to show her true colours—as soon as she'd lost interest in my dad, I wasn't even worth speaking to.

Not that I cared, of course. I hardly gave her another thought as I finished typing the meeting notes and sent them to Amanda. She was as pleased as I'd expected with the way I'd played up her role. She didn't even mention the fact that the attendance list included what was probably fewer than half of the kids who'd been there.

It was getting close to the end of the therapy session so I didn't bother starting on my homework. What I did do was gather all the courage I could scrape together and compose a text to Dennis. It took a few (fourteen) tries before I was satisfied.

Hey Dennis. If you need someone to help you do something for one of the old folks on your street let me know.

Totally innocent, right? No way could he read anything into that. He could only think I was a super-nice person, eager to do things for others. Which, is apparently what he *did* think. His answer came back in no time.

Awesome Zoey! If you're free after lunch this Saturday I know someone who could really use our help.

My heart took off ka-thumping in a wild celebration. Dennis Fuller had (more or less) said that I was awesome. And we'd be spending hours together on Saturday. It wasn't quite a date—but it could easily lead to one! I couldn't stop smiling as I sent my answer.

Count me in.

There was just one problem. I already had plans that day.

Thirteen

"Something wrong, honey?"

Dad's question on the drive home alerted me to the fact that I was accidentally giving away information. My face has been known to send out signals, which Dad pounces on like a starving cat on a mouse.

"Nope," I said.

"You look a little troubled. Sure nothing is bothering you?"

"No. I'm good."

"It's never a good idea to push our feelings down," he said.

Oh, brother. I knew from experience that this parental prodding could go on for quite a while. There are times when it's actually easier to *have* a conversation with my dad than it is to *avoid* one.

"I kind of double-booked myself on Saturday," I said.

"You made separate plans with Bean and Jenna?"

"No, Dad. I have more than two friends, you know."

"Right. Of course you do." I hope he sounds more convincing than that when he's reassuring his patients. Otherwise, no one is ever going to get better.

"Bean and his girlfriend won't care if I back out," I continued, "but Jenna's another story."

"*Bean* has a *girlfriend*? Is that new?"

"Very new." I'd never told Dad about the girlfriend-boyfriend phase Bean and I had gone through, which spared me from the kind of awkward questions I'd have been in for if he'd known about it.

"Interesting," he said. I didn't ask what he meant by that. "So, you're worried that this will be a problem with Jenna?"

"It might be." More like one hundred and fifty percent for sure. It's not that Jenna's unreasonable, and all we were going to do was hang out at the mall, but her addiction to organization makes her react badly to change.

I thought about what to do while Dad made

a couple of lame suggestions. I pretended to listen, and even nodded and smiled a couple of times, but the poor man is totally out of touch with the way my generation communicates.

"Thanks, Dad," I said when he'd finally wrapped up. He *beamed*. And for the record, I was being sincere—not because his advice was helpful, but because he means well.

Once I'd pretended to agree to Dad's idea (which had something to do with an open, honest conversation in which I'd let Jenna know that I respect her feelings—blah, blah, blah) I came up with a plan of my own. I would ignore everything he'd suggested and put my own strategy in place. I'd lie.

I texted Bean—taking the safest route.

Change of plans for Saturday. Can't meet up until after 4.

His answer was back in a few seconds.

What's happening before 4?

I'll be busy do-gooding my way into Dennis Fuller's heart.

Okay, that's what I *thought*. My actual reply was a little less truthful.

I have to do something with my mom. Let Jenna know. My phone is about to die.

That was how I lined up Bean to take the heat, and gave Jenna time to cool off before I had to face her. It would have worked perfectly if it hadn't been for Bean.

Not that Jenna wasn't still a little grumpy about having to rearrange her day. She was. But it was Bean who really stirred things up. He was alone when he joined us at lunch, and I might have irked him when I asked how he'd managed to make it to the table without Mariska to hold him up.

"Ow, my si—" he started, then cut himself off. His eyes narrowed.

"Hey, how come you couldn't do whatever with your mom on Sunday instead of messing up Jenna's plans?" he said. "That was pretty rude."

"Yeah, Zoey. What was wrong with Sunday?" Jenna asked. She flashed Bean a grateful smile for being so considerate of her feelings. It was as if she'd never met him before.

"I, uh ..." I said, thinking frantically. I managed to spit out some garbled half-words that sounded as though I was mumbling under-water. Not exactly a convincing performance. And Bean wasn't letting up.

"Well, Zoey?" he asked, just as Mariska reached the table and slipped in beside him.

"Well, what?" she asked, looking from him to Jenna and me and back.

"My mother needs me for a while tomorrow," I said sadly. "That's why they're mad at me for changing our plans."

To my astonishment, Mariska was instantly outraged.

"*What?*" she said. "Are you kidding me? Zoey doesn't get to spend that much time with her mom—I can't believe you guys are giving her a hard time about something like that."

Then she elbowed Bean, gave Jenna a reproachful look, and that was the end of that discussion.

Early Saturday afternoon I was at Dennis's front door.

Gary opened it. Of course. He arched an eyebrow, winked at me in the creepiest possible way and said, "I've been working on my flirting techniques. How am I doing?"

I giggled, remembering how I'd told him he was bad at flirting.

"Come on. Scale of one to ten, what would you give me?" he said, grinning.

I shuddered. "Believe me," I told him, "there's no scale for what you just did."

Gary put his head back and laughed out loud. Then he grinned and made a wide sweep with his hand to usher me inside.

"*Entrez-vous, mademoiselle.*"

"*Merci, monsieur,*" I said, stepping into the hall. Keeping Gary as an ally was in my best interests, but I was also genuinely starting to like him. He'd been a stand-up guy after I'd made a fool of myself, plus he was friendly and fun.

Dennis appeared at the end of the hall, an apple in his hand. He waved it in greeting as he came toward me and I saw that a huge hunk was missing from one side. Judging by the bulge in his cheek, the whole, enormous bite was in his mouth.

"Excuse my brother," Gary said. "He hasn't eaten in weeks."

"Mftmft," Dennis said. A small piece of apple flew out as he was trying to speak. He caught it, looked down at it resting in the palm of his hand and held it out like he was offering it to Gary, then to me.

"Tempting," I said. "If only I hadn't had such a big lunch."

Dennis laughed, which caused more apple bits to fly and prompted Gary to offer me an umbrella.

A few minutes later, mess cleaned up, Dennis and I were walking, side by side, down his street. It was a good feeling, to be with him. I let myself imagine how much more thrilling it would be if we were an actual couple.

"The woman we're going to help out—Mrs. Wibberley—has lived on this street ever since I can remember," Dennis told me. "She's been all alone since her husband died a couple of years ago."

"Doesn't she have any kids to do stuff for her?"

"There's a daughter, but she lives on the west coast." He paused then, and his eyes grew sad. "I suppose the reason I feel so strongly about this is that I had a grandmother I hardly ever saw because she lived so far away. Then, at her funeral, we heard about how some kids from her neighbourhood had stepped up and taken care of things she couldn't do herself."

"So you're kind of paying it forward," I said.

Dennis glanced at me with a faint smile. "I guess I am," he said.

We were turning up the walk to her house by then, and neither of us spoke again until the door opened in answer to our knock. Mrs. Wibberley, I presumed. I'd been picturing a frail, little old lady type with her grey hair in a bun. The woman in the doorway, though elderly, was on the plump side, and her hair had recently seen some kind of henna rinse.

She peered at us for a minute, half frowning. Then her face lit up as she recognized Dennis.

"You're that nice boy from the house with the lovely red oak tree."

"I hope so, ma'am," Dennis said. "I mean, I hope I'm nice—I know where I live."

She smiled at that before turning her attention to me. "And is this your girlfriend?"

"Oh, I'm sure she has better taste than that," Dennis said. He gave me a quick look of apology, as if I'd been horribly insulted. "This is Zoey. We belong to a group of teen volunteers, and we were wondering if there might be something we could do for you for an hour or two this afternoon."

Mrs. Wibberley's hand flew to her mouth. "Oh, my!" she said. It made me a little nervous, probably because of my experience with Chantal the frequent crier, but Mrs. Wibberley managed not to burst into tears.

"Why, I scarcely know what to say," she told us. "Just yesterday I was wondering how on earth I was going to get the backyard ready for winter."

"Well, now you can consider it done," Dennis said.

We followed Mrs. Wibberley as she led us behind the house. She hunted around for a key to the padlock on her shed, and then opened it to reveal shovels and tools, along with an assortment of broken stuff that I doubted anyone was ever going to fix.

Cleaning up the yard looked like a quick job when we started but it took us about two hours to get everything done. We put the patio furniture in the shed, raked and bagged the leaves, covered a couple of bushes for the winter, cut back some dead plants in the garden and cleaned the brick barbeque. Dennis scrubbed the grill with a wire brush while I used the hose to wash out a metal container, half full of dirt, and a couple of encrusted flowerpots.

I was winding the hose onto its holder when Mrs. Wibberley came out the back door. She clapped her hands and said the yard looked wonderful. I had to agree—you wouldn't believe what a difference a few hours of work had made.

"I can't thank the two of you enough for everything you've done," she said. She crossed over to the barbeque, smiling back and forth at me and Dennis. And then she said, "I guess this is as good a time as any to bring Charlie in for the winter."

I froze in horror as she reached for the metal container I'd just hosed clean.

"Charlie always loved being out in the backyard," she said sadly. "And barbeque! My gracious sakes, he just couldn't get enough of it. That's why I always put him out here in the summer."

I tried to speak. Nothing came out.

"Then, of course, I bring him back inside in the fall," she continued. "It's such a comfort to have my dear Charlie ..."

Her voice trailed off and she looked down at the object in her hands. A confused frown settled on her face, and I knew she was only seconds away from grasping the terrible fact that the container she was holding no longer held Charlie—or anything else.

"I'm so sorry!" I blurted. "I didn't know that was an urn."

Mrs. Wibberley's mouth fell open. Her trembling hand lifted the lid from Charlie's last resting place (well, second last) and she peered inside.

"He's *gone*," she said weakly. She refocused,

her eyes narrowing as they settled on me. "*Where* is Charlie?" she demanded.

I wished I didn't have to tell her, but she deserved the truth. I cleared my throat.

"You're standing in him, ma'am."

Mrs. Wibberley looked down. She was wearing sturdy white shoes, the kind you see on hospital workers. They were planted squarely in a half inch of grey sludge.

"Oh, *dear*," Mrs. Wibberley said faintly. "My poor, dear Charlie."

Thankfully, Dennis stepped forward then and took her arm. "Let me get you into the house," he said.

I stood, mortified, as she pulled her feet out of Charlie's soggy ashes and allowed Dennis to lead her back across the yard. I didn't see whether or not she wiped the grey muck from her shoes before she went into the house.

It's hard to say how long I stood there, my head swimming with mental images I could have done without. This was easily the worst thing I'd ever done in my life. *Poor* Mrs. Wibberley. The most horrible part was knowing there was nothing I could ever do to make it right.

I guess I *could* have tried to scrape old Charlie up and plop globs of him back into the urn, but the thought of doing that made my skin crawl. It was bad enough looking at the sodden grey patch on the ground. Even the *thought* of touching it sent a shivery shudder through me.

"Cold?"

I glanced up and saw that Dennis had returned. His one-word question made me realize that I was trembling.

"Not cold, no. Horrified, yes. Embarrassed, definitely."

"It's not the end of the world," he said. "I had a talk with her—kind of got her to see that Charlie would rather be free in a place he loved than closed up in a metal jar."

"Really?"

"I swear. She'll be fine." He reached across the space between us and touched my arm, which made my eyes fill with tears.

"Hey, don't be so hard on yourself," he said softly. "You didn't do it on purpose."

"Of course I didn't. But it's still my fault that her husband's ashes are all over the ground."

"What?" Dennis blinked a couple of times, then he smothered a laugh.

"How can you possibly find that funny?"

"Because her husband is buried in Peaceful Pines Cemetery. Charlie was her Saint Bernard."

Fourteen

"Charlie is a *dog*?"

"Yup," Dennis said. "Or, actually, he *was* a dog. At the moment, he's a mound of mud."

"Sorry, Charlie," I said, giving what was left of his remains an apologetic glance before turning back toward Dennis. His eyes danced with amusement.

"We'd better get out of here," he said. "I'm gonna lose it any second."

There was no coaxing required. We hurried down the driveway and along the street toward Dennis's place, barely making it out of sight of Mrs. Wibberley's house before he exploded with laughter.

"You thought you dumped out her *husband*!" Dennis said, wiping the corners of his eyes.

"And that she was *standing* on him," I said.

The image, so horrifying just moments earlier, now seemed hilarious.

"You mean standing *in* him."

Okay, so maybe we were being a little insensitive. We didn't mean anything by it—at least I know *I* didn't. It was just one of those situations where something strikes you as funny and you *cannot* get yourself back under control.

Unless, of course, you happen to look across the street and see a terrifying mask of fury staring at you, which is what I saw when Stephanie Roth's face appeared, hovering there like something straight out of a horror movie.

My throat was instantly dry and tight, my laughter silenced. Dennis looked at me curiously, and then turned to see what I was staring at.

And, of course, there was an instant transformation. The psycho was gone, and in her place Stephanie stood smiling, waving and calling, "Hey, you guys!" in the friendliest tone you ever heard.

"Hey, Steph!" Dennis answered. "What's up?"

"I just got back from 'lending a hand' to a single mom," she said.

"That's great—we were helping someone too. Only not for the Lend a Hand group. It was just something we did on our own."

"Me too, actually. The group seems to be

taking forever to get organized, so I found something myself." She flashed a big smile that practically screamed *I'm such a phony!*

Sadly, it was plain to see that Dennis was buying it. I, on the other hand, could see right through her. Besides, I remembered her talking to him right after the Lend a Hand meeting. He'd probably told her the same things he told me that night—that the meeting had been a waste of time, and that he wanted to do something meaningful. Now here she was, putting on a big act to convince him that she was sweet and caring and dedicated to helping others.

"Was your good deed nearby?" I asked.

"Uh, *no-oo*," Stephanie said. I hoped that Dennis had noticed the way she drew it out into two snarky syllables.

"I just thought that might be why you were here." I had her now! It would be hard for Dennis to miss the fact that she was chasing him. With any luck, her excuse for hanging around his street would be super-lame.

Stephanie smirked at Dennis as if they were in on a private joke.

"Nope," she said.

"I guess you have *some other reason* for being here, then," I said, with a worried glance at Dennis. It didn't look like his boy brain was cluing in. On the other hand, Stephanie *had* to know what I was up to, but instead of getting rattled, she laughed. Her next words explained why.

"Well, yeah. I *live* here."

"Her house is practically right across from mine," Dennis said helpfully.

"Oh," I said. In a small voice.

"And what about *you*, Zoey?" Stephanie asked. Before I could answer, she looked at Dennis and said, "Wait—I know. *You* must have asked Zoey to come over and help you. Right?"

"Actually, Zoey offered," Dennis said. He smiled at me.

I forced myself to smile back. *I* knew, and *Stephanie* knew, that I'd just been scorched at my own game. But *Dennis* still seemed completely oblivious to the undercurrents between us and, at that point, the best I could hope for was to keep it that way.

"Well, wasn't that *nice* of you, Zoey," Stephanie said with a smirk. "Couldn't you find anyone who needed help near your own place?"

"I like to help out anywhere I can," I said. My face hurt from the frozen smile, and I knew it was time to get out of there before things went any further downhill. I made an excuse and beat a hasty retreat. I might as well have been waving a white flag.

On my way home I decided I was definitely letting go of the silly ideas about Dennis and me. As a couple, that is. Knowing that a crazed psycho lived across the street from him was enough to convince me it was time to forget this guy.

It was over before it even started.

Don't ask me how I didn't see this coming, but I managed to make it through the rest of the weekend and a whole school day without it even once occurring to me that Stephanie might cause trouble.

It wasn't until after the final bell on Monday that I discovered what a mistake *that* had been. I was standing in the bus loading area with Jenna, Bean and Mariska when I heard, "Well, well, well. If it isn't Little Miss Do-gooder."

A shiver of panic ran through me as I recognized Stephanie's voice.

I whirled around. So did my friends. She treated us to a sneer, put her hands on her hips, squared her shoulders and stuck her chin out in front of her. If that was meant to be intimidating, I have to say she nailed it.

"Don't you have anything better to do than bother me?" Not one of my top ten comebacks, but it isn't easy to stay on your game when you're staring in the face of raging lunacy.

She smirked. "Sure, but I thought you might like to know what Dennis told me after you left on Saturday."

My next brilliant response was to flap my mouth a couple of times. While I performed this amazing feat, I sensed Bean and Jenna shifting their attention from Stephanie to me.

"That's right," Stephanie sneered, stepping closer. "I heard all about what you did with the dog's ashes. Now *that* was impressive. I'm wondering if I should warn Destiny that there are signs you're staging a takeover as club president."

My face was on fire but my tongue remained frozen, so I did the only thing I could do. I turned my back on her and walked away. It actually felt kind of good, even with Stephanie's crazy laughter chasing me.

Half a block later I heard running steps behind me and Jenna calling my name. I stopped, head down, and waited for her to catch up. I knew there'd be questions to answer, and she didn't waste any time before she hurled the first one at me.

"You want to tell me what *that* was about?"

"Where's Bean?"

"Oh, don't worry—he's coming," she said (like that might be good news). "Mariska's bus was pulling in when I left, so he won't be far behind me."

"Can we just wait for him? I don't want to do this twice."

"Whatever." Jenna shrugged. She looked disgusted, and I couldn't blame her.

It wasn't long—maybe a couple of minutes—before Bean's frosted head came bobbing along the street. He didn't look quite as angry as Jenna, but you can't always tell with Bean.

"Okay, we're both here," Jenna said.

"I can see that."

"*Really?* You think this is a good time to give us attitude?"

"Sorry." I took a deep breath, looked at Jenna, then at Bean, and didn't know where to start. "What do you want to know?"

"You didn't go to your mom's on Saturday, did you?" Jenna said.

"No."

"You made that up so you could ditch us to do something with Dennis."

"Yes."

"And you joined that stupid club of Destiny's, didn't you?" Bean finally spoke. I knew that was going to be the thing that bothered him the most.

"Kind of. I guess. Honestly, it all sort of just happened. I didn't want to join the club—but I had the crazy idea that Dennis might be, you know, interested in me."

"So, you've been lying to us for, what, *weeks?*"

"I didn't look at it that way, until this weekend. It was more like I was keeping some things to myself."

There was a long moment of silence while their eyes burned into me. I braced myself for the blast that I knew would be coming. But when Bean spoke, it wasn't at all what I was expecting.

"You like him a lot, huh?"

I met his eyes for the first time since the conversation began. "I guess, but that wasn't going anywhere anyway. He was just being friendly. Besides, I don't want to have to deal with Stephanie."

I didn't bother saying how awful I felt that Dennis had told her about Charlie's ashes. Normally, that would be the kind of thing I'd have talked over with them, but it didn't seem like the right time to be reaching out for support and comfort.

"That girl is seriously off balance," Jenna said.

"No kidding. Did you see her eyes back there?" Bean asked.

"I doubt she'll be bothering me again," I said.

"But to be safe, I'll make sure she knows I plan to keep away from Dennis."

"Why should you have to do that?" Bean said. "*She* should learn to turn the crazy down."

"Like that's ever going to happen. But you know what? I don't even care any more. I'm just sorry for lying to you guys."

"Forget it," Bean said, because he's a guy and that's forgiveness male-style.

Jenna was a slightly different story.

She told me how much I'd hurt her. I said I was really, truly, very, very sorry.

She told me she never would have thought I'd do something like that to them. I hung my head in shame.

She reminded me how much doing Random Acts with her two best friends meant to her, and how betrayed she felt that I'd joined Lend a Hand. I swore that *our* group meant a lot to me too and that the other one meant *nothing*.

She pointed out how important trust and honesty are in a friendship. By then I thought this whole thing had been going on long enough, so I said I understood if she didn't want to be friends any more, let my shoulders slump in dejection, turned and began to walk away.

"Don't go," Jenna said, with just the perfect touch of drama in her voice. I lifted my head

slowly, looked back and saw her smile of forgiveness. Then we hugged and that was over with.

Forgiveness female-style.

I've got to say, it was a good feeling to know I
wouldn't be hiding things from them any more.
The mess of the last few weeks was behind me
and that was that.

As if anything is ever that easy.

Fifteen

I made up my mind about a few things as I was getting ready for school Tuesday morning. True, a lot had been going wrong, but I wasn't going to let that get me down. The smartest way to handle problems is to pick yourself up and make a fresh start. That's exactly what I was doing.

If I'd been Jenna, I'd have made a colour-coded spreadsheet of some sort—maybe a few pie charts and a mission statement. But I wasn't, so I settled for making a mental list, which went like this:

1. Forget Dennis. He wasn't interested in me in the first place, and besides, he blabbed about the dog's ashes to Psycho Stephanie.

2. Drop out of the Lend a Hand group.
   (Not much of a sacrifice, considering I'm
   at the top of their Most Wanted list.)
3. Make it up to Bean and Jenna—for all
   the lies and sneaky stuff I've pulled lately.
4. Put an honest effort into my random acts
   of kindness.

Ever since Saturday, I'd been seeing Random
Acts differently. Sure, I'd messed up some of
the things I'd done—so what? That didn't mean
I wanted to give up. Not after helping out
Mrs. Wibberley.

Yes, there had been that unfortunate business
with Charlie's remains, but everything else
about helping the old lady had been good. The
expression on her face when Dennis told her we
were going to clean the yard for her—that was
something I wasn't going to forget. But the best
feeling came when we were doing the actual
work. Knowing we were saving a fragile old
woman from struggling with things that would
have been so hard for her—that was awesome.
We really *had* made a difference for someone.

The idea for what I could do for my next
random act came to me as I hurried past the
Kimuras' house on the way to school. It was
brilliant—a chance to redeem myself—and I

loved it instantly. Then, I realized I'd never be able to do it alone. It was only doable if I could persuade someone to help me.

I ruled out Jenna instantly. There was no way she'd be up for this—smuggling cookies into the teachers' lounge was about as daring as she was ever going to get.

That left Bean. The problem with Bean wouldn't be nerve, it would be motivation. I'd need to think of some way to lure him in, and it would have to be strong enough to overcome his natural laziness—a powerful force in its own right.

I thought about it all day, but came up with nothing. And then, right after school, a solution fell into my hands.

Mariska had just stepped onto her bus (waiting with her was getting to be a routine for us) when Bean turned to Jenna and me and blurted, "I told Mariska about our random acts thing."

"Bean!" said Jenna. "We all *promised* to keep it a secret!"

"Yeah, but Destiny was trying to get Mariska to join Lend a Hand—and she was talking like she might do it."

"So, what you're really saying is you didn't just tell her about it, you actually told her she could join us."

"I might have told her something like that."

Jenna stared at Bean until he couldn't meet her eyes any more. As soon as he looked away, she shrugged. "Fine. It's done now, but I hope *she* can keep *her* mouth shut."

"She can, and she will," Bean said, like the short time they'd been dating had been more than enough for him to get to know everything about her.

"While we're on the subject," Jenna said, "what random acts have *you* done so far? I know what I did, and Zoey says she's done a few and has others in mind, but I can't seem to think of a single thing you've done."

"It's been hard to come up with anything," Bean said. "Don't tell Mariska, though. I don't want her to get the wrong idea about me."

"What wrong idea is that?" I asked.

"You know—I don't want her to think I'm the kind of guy who doesn't keep his promises."

"You *don't* keep your promises," I said.

"Yeah, but I'm going to."

"Then you'd better get started," Jenna said.

And there it was—my chance to rope him in.

"Actually, that reminds me—I have a random act that I want to do, but it's going to take two people. If you ask nicely, I'll let you in on it."

Bean remained silent.

"Or, maybe I should ask Mariska. I've been meaning to have a chat with her anyway. She's probably curious about *why* you're so against Destiny's group."

I let the threat of the skid-mark story hang in the air. Bean threw up his hands in surrender.

"Okay, you've got me cornered. What would I have to do?"

I hesitated. If I told him now, he'd have three days to think of an excuse to back out. So I said, "Meet me at my place on Friday. I'll fill you in then. We need to do it after dark, so don't make any other plans that evening."

"I thought this was your weekend at your mom's," Bean said.

"She's working late on Friday, so I'm not going over until Saturday morning," I told him. "And stop trying to get out of it."

"Can Mariska come?"

"No. But it's something cool, so she'll be super-impressed when you tell her about it."

"You can drop the sales pitch—I *said* I'd do it. What time do I have to be there?"

"Just before dark," I said, pleased that it had turned out to be that easy to enlist his help. Soon, I'd be making up for the misunderstanding over the Kimuras' newspaper. Maybe someday, I'd be able to walk past their house without staring straight ahead to avoid their accusing eyes.

I was feeling super-positive that things were falling into place when I settled in at my desk at Therapy Solutions that evening. And then Glenda came in and my good mood vanished.

She couldn't have looked more like a woman on the hunt for a husband if she'd had a marriage licence in one hand and a pen in the other. Fake eyelashes, *waaaay* too much makeup, and her sweater was so tight I'm surprised she could breathe.

I did my best not to look bothered as she gave me a smile and a wave and then settled into a chair. The worst thing was, I knew right away that it was my own fault. I'd slackened off on the secret admirer messages after they seemed to have worked. Glenda had started coming in looking frumpy and I'd decided my father was out of danger. Obviously, I was wrong, and now look what had happened!

It was time to rekindle the fake romance in Glenda's life. The second the group went into the session room I started composing a new anonymous note. It had to be a good one, so I took my time.

> *Perhaps you are thinking that I have*
> *forgotten you? Do not worry—that will*
> *never happen! I think of you every moment,*
> *from the second I open my eyes in the*
> *morning until I close them again at night.*
> *Even when I'm asleep, you are in my dreams.*
> *You are everything to me. I can hardly wait*
> *to be with you. You are my destiny and we*
> *WILL be together some day soon. I will*
> *always be your Secret Admirer.*

I read it over a couple of times. Not to brag, but it was awesome. It oozed romance and was practically guaranteed to shift her attention away from my dad. The only problem was that it was a temporary solution. When time went by and the secret admirer never showed up, she'd probably go right back to flaunting her sweaters in front of my father again.

After I'd slipped outside, folded the note and tucked it under the windshield wiper of her car, I gave that some more thought. I had to find a way to convince her that my dad was the *last* person she'd ever want to date or marry. But that wasn't turning out to be as easy as I'd expected. She'd already heard me describe my father as a child-hater who let his daughter go out with shockingly inappropriate guys. If that wasn't enough to put her off, what would it take?

And then it came to me. The answer was so obvious I was embarrassed I hadn't thought of it sooner. I could hardly wait for the session to end, and I crossed my fingers that I'd have a chance to talk to her.

Sometimes you have to make your own luck, which is what I did when the group finished up and filed out of the therapy room. As they gathered at the coat rack, I got Glenda's attention and beckoned her over.

"Hi, Zoey," she said when she'd crossed back over to my desk. "What's up?"

"I was wondering if you got a babysitter," I said. I'd been wondering no such thing, but I needed to draw her into an innocent conversation before I unleashed the new plan to put her off my dad.

"Oh. That's really thoughtful of you," she said. "As a matter of fact—"

A burst of laughter from the other end of the room broke into our conversation. We looked over to see Bill, red-faced and struggling out of Glenda's coat, which was miles too small for him.

"G-g-g-getting in t-t-t-touch with your

f-f-f-feminine side?" Sonny teased as Bill tugged the jacket off and hung it back on the rack. His face was a deep shade of purple.

"Easy mistake," Glenda said. "Our jackets are almost the exact same shade of brown—I've almost put Bill's on a few times myself."

That earned her a sheepish smile from Bill, who grabbed his own coat and hurried out without even putting it on.

"He's so easily embarrassed," Glenda said softly, so the others couldn't hear. "Anyway, you were asking if I got a babysitter."

"Right. One of my friends might be interested—I'm not sure because I didn't want to ask her until I knew if you still needed someone."

"I appreciate that but I think I've got it covered. My friend's daughter has been helping out, and I've got a few people to interview this week, so I'm probably all right for the time being."

"Okay," I said. Then I covered my mouth with my hand and pretended to be hiding a huge yawn. "Sorry—one of Dad's girlfriends was over really late last night and she had the TV on so loud I couldn't get to sleep."

"*One* of your dad's girlfriends?" Glenda echoed.

"Mm-hmm," I said innocently. "I think he has

three right now. It could even be four. It's hard to keep track."

Glenda blinked. I could practically see her thinking that she should drop it, but she couldn't stop herself from asking, "And that's *normal* for him?"

"Oh, sure," I said, making sure I kept my voice casual. "I think that might be why my parents split up—he's too free-spirited to be tied down to just one woman."

Glenda opened her mouth, drew in a breath slowly, and then closed it again. She cleared her throat and said, "Thanks again for asking about my babysitter situation." Then she reached across the desk and gave my hand a quick squeeze before crossing the floor to the coat rack, slinging on her jacket and hurrying out the door.

I could hardly keep from laughing out loud. It was perfect! What a genius I was. There was no way she'd ever want to throw herself at my father again.

Sixteen

I was eager to see how well my plan was working, so it was disappointing when Thursday came and there was a note from Miss Barducci saying Glenda had cancelled. That meant it would be Tuesday before I'd see what kind of effect the shocking news about what a humungous woman-izer my dad was had on her. I was expecting to see a lot less makeup, and clothes that weren't so flirty.

I suppose describing my own father like that wasn't the nicest thing to do, especially when he hardly dates at all and actually seems to still be kind of hung up on my mom. But I couldn't waste time worrying about that. Besides, it was for his own protection, so it wasn't *really* all that wrong. If you know what I mean.

And then it was Friday. I reminded Bean after school about his promise and he showed up just before 8:30 without even trying to get out of it.

"So, what's the big secret?" he asked.

"This is an idea I got from what Dennis and I did last weekend," I said. "And it's also to make up for something that I did by accident to one of my neighbours."

I wasn't especially eager to tell him the details, but I also knew there was no way he'd go along with tonight's plan unless he had the entire story. A few minutes later, I'd filled him in on the whole sad newspaper fiasco. Bean seemed to find it quite entertaining.

"Very bad girl," he laughed. "Very bad girl."

I wasn't exactly amused, but at least Bean found himself entertaining. He wagged his finger and shook his head and made a variety of strange faces that had nothing to do with anything as far as I could tell.

"Okay, that'll do. At least I was making an effort."

He snickered. "So, your philosophy must be that a bad deed is better than no deed."

"Don't make me hurt you, Bean."

He didn't quite stop laughing, but I like to think it took on a kind of nervous sound.

"Okay, so here's what we're going to do,"

I said. "We're going to rake their yard, bag the leaves and take them away."

"What?"

"You heard me."

"You want us to rake someone's yard *in the dark!*"

"That's right. It's the only way we can do it secretly." I didn't bother to mention that Mr. Kimura still stopped whatever he was doing, crossed his arms and glared at me anytime he saw me pass by.

Bean was staring. I gave him a cheery smile and said, "It'll be fun. And think how impressed Mariska will be when you tell her what an awesome thing you did—in the dark—to make an old couple happy."

I could tell he was giving it some thought. Time to seal the deal.

"Anyway, you said you would, so you can't back out now."

"Fine." He frowned, but it changed to a grin after a second. "When do we start?"

"We can probably go now—their lights go out super-early. I think they go to bed at 8:00 or something."

"You have leaf bags?"

"Dad always buys way more than we need. I'll run downstairs and grab some."

Ten minutes later we were armed with rakes and bags and a flashlight, in case the street light wasn't bright enough to see what we were doing when we got to the backyard. We started in the front and worked our way around behind the house.

I guess we were an interesting sight. Everyone who passed by on the sidewalk slowed down and gawked at us. I was surprised that no one stopped or came right out and asked why we were raking leaves in the dark. We got a few amused looks from people who probably thought someone was making us do it as some kind of peculiar punishment.

Being stared at was no problem, but there was one thing that worried me. The noise! You would not *believe* the racket those leaves made. The crackling and crunching and general ruckus was enough to snap someone out of a coma. But there wasn't a sign of anyone stirring in the Kimura house. The worst was when we were stuffing leaves into bags—and still, no one flicked on a light or pulled back a curtain or gave us any other reason to think we'd disturbed them.

It took nearly two hours. Don't think Bean wasn't fed up by then, because he definitely *was*, but he wasn't quite brave enough to walk off and leave me to finish the job by myself. Of course,

I couldn't have stopped him if he'd decided to do that. On the other hand, he'd have paid for it later—and he knew it. So, whenever he gave me a long, mournful look to let me know he'd rather be just about anywhere else on the planet, I hissed, "Don't even think about it!" and he dropped his head and went back to work.

"I sure hope we got every single leaf," Bean grumbled as we carried the jam-packed bags to the designated community pickup one street over. "I'm worried we might have missed one."

"We might have. Maybe you should go back and check," I said. That shut him up. I admit that I'd probably been a little too fussy, but I wanted Mr. and Mrs. Kimura to be utterly amazed at the job we'd done. I wished I could be there to see their faces when they opened their curtains to the sight of a lovely, clean yard in the morning.

We dropped the bags off and headed to my place, since Dad had promised to drive Bean home when we got back. (I didn't think Dad would let me skulk around someone's yard after dark that way, so I'd pretended we were going to Jenna's to play video games.)

As we walked along, I asked Bean how it felt to have done his very first random act.

"I'm delirious with joy," he said. Then he snorted, in case I'd missed the sarcasm.

I didn't care. The important thing was that my fresh start had kicked in with an awesome random act. I was feeling good about it. It was unfortunate that it had to be anonymous because I really would have liked them to know I wasn't the thieving troublemaker they believed I was.

As I thought about that, I decided it probably wouldn't hurt to give them some sort of hint. Nothing totally obvious—just enough so they'd *suspect* it was me. A wink, a wave, a hint of a smile. They might even come right out and ask me if I did it, and of course I wouldn't actually *say* I did, but I could answer in a way that would kind of confirm it for them.

That probably sounds as though I was looking for credit, but I figured it would really be for *their* sakes. After all, here's this frail old couple living a few houses away from someone they think is some sort of newspaper-stealing maniac. Finding out I was actually the kind of person who would clean up all their leaves in the middle of the night would do a lot to put their minds at rest.

In the meantime, my body was ready for a good snooze after all that work. I crawled into bed feeling pleased and proud and was in a deep, contented sleep in no time.

The next morning I woke to the promising sound of Dad singing in the kitchen, which almost always means that he's making pancakes! I stuck my feet into my slippers, made a quick bathroom stop and hurried to the breakfast nook.

"Do you want blueberries or chocolate chips in yours?" he asked.

"No thanks—just plain." I put the cutlery and plates on the table while Dad poured batter into the skillet. He doesn't believe in sissy pancakes—each one nearly fills the bottom of the frying pan, which means he can only cook one at a time. By the time he'd flipped it golden side up, I'd gotten out the butter and syrup and poured us glasses of milk. There was nothing left for me to do then but plunk myself down and wait. Seconds later, Dad delivered the first golden-brown beauty to me.

It smelled delicious. I buttered it and added syrup, barely listening to Dad's stream of conversation, which tends to keep on going long after you've stopped listening.

"I was out for a walk earlier—we've had so many warm days this fall, it would be a shame not to take advantage, and there's nothing like a brisk walk in the morning to give a person energy for the day. This will be a busy one, too—there's grocery shopping, and I've got to make an appointment to have the winter tires put on the car before the first snow. It's good to be ready before you actually need them, and winter will be here before we know it."

Groceries and tires. Did he seriously expect me to pay attention to his plans when they were that boring? My thoughts began to drift to things a person might actually care about while Dad's voice faded to a drone in the background. It was pure luck that the next thing he said penetrated my brain at all.

"In fact, I noticed the Blakes have already wrapped their rose bushes, and Phil Jindra was putting away his lawn lights when I passed by. He stopped to talk for a bit. Told me a funny story about his wife getting a call from Mrs. Kimura. She was complaining that their leaves had been stolen."

"*What?*"

Dad laughed a bit before saying, "Strange, right? Seems that someone took all the leaves out of their yard during the night. According to Phil, Mr. Kimura actually called the police about it."

I felt my eyes get big and round. Dad laughed again.

"Imagine calling the police—over leaves! Somehow, I don't think they'll be putting a team of detectives on the case."

I laughed weakly, then said, "But ... *why* would they be upset about that?"

"Beats me. I'd be overjoyed if someone made off with our leaves. But not the Kimuras. For some reason, they *wanted* theirs."

That was the end of my appetite. I managed a few more nibbles, but when Dad went to pour more batter into the frying pan for himself I scraped the rest of my pancake into the garbage.

"I'm going to get my stuff ready for when Mom gets here."

"Okey-doke. Oh, and Zoey—"

"Yeah?"

"Don't steal any leaves on the way." He winked and laughed heartily as he flipped the pancake.

If only he knew.

Seventeen

A text pinged on my phone as I was tossing my bag into Mom's car.

You busy tonight?

Dennis. He had a lot of nerve messaging me after blabbing to Stephanie about my little mistake with the dog's ashes. I'd avoided him at school all week (not that he'd been falling over himself trying to talk to me), but now here he was, texting me like everything was fine. Some people don't catch on very fast, that's for sure.

I decided not to answer him. It wouldn't have surprised me if he'd thought he could talk me into helping him clean up someone else's yard so he could get all the credit and then turn around and spread stories to make me look like a mental case afterward. That was probably what he wanted. Or maybe it was about a stupid Lend a Hand meeting—like I was ever going to another one of those.

Of course, he didn't *know* I was through with that. Maybe I should tell him. Or check to see if there was some other reason he was texting me. Like, what if I'd dropped something in Mrs. Wibberley's yard? Or what if he wanted to apologize? Maybe he wanted to ask me out. Not that I would *go*, of course. Unless he had a really good explanation for why he'd told Stephanie about Charlie's ashes.

"Earth to Zoey."

"Huh? Oh, sorry, Mom. I was just thinking about something."

"Your homework?"

"Of course. What else could it be?"

Mom snickered. "My second guess was going to be a boy. If I hadn't got it right the first time, that is."

"Nope, you were dead-on."

She glanced at me, raised an eyebrow and said, "Well, don't forget that I'm always here if you need to talk about 'homework,' or anything else."

"I know, Mom." And I did, but this wasn't something I was interested in talking about. Not just because it was complicated, but because admitting the way I'd let myself get sucked in, and knowing I'd been talked about behind my back—none of it felt like anything I wanted to tell to anyone. I changed the subject.

"Are we doing anything with Ray this weekend?"

Mom cleared her throat. "Actually, Ray and I aren't seeing each other any more."

Okay, I admit that the first thought that flashed into my head was: *Maybe my mom and dad will get back together.* It was an automatic thing, as if the thought had been there, waiting to spring up like some kind of child-of-divorce's jack-in-the-box. Thankfully, my mouth didn't blurt out anything that stupid to my mother.

"Did you guys have a fight?"

Mom smiled, as if she was genuinely amused. "Not really," she said. "I mean, we argued sometimes, but this wasn't over anything like that."

As she signalled and slowed the car for a turn, Mom took a deep breath and let it out slowly. I could tell she was trying to make up her mind about what to tell me, and I've learned that the less I push for information, the more she's likely to say. So, I stayed quiet, and after a minute she said, "You know that Ray was married before, right? Well, he and his wife never formalized things when they broke up. Technically, they're still married, even though they've been apart for three years."

A bad feeling crept over me then because I knew where this was going.

"Anyway, they've been talking lately, and they're thinking they might try again."

"So he dumps you, just like that, to run back to his wife?" I blurted. Normally, I'd have been a bit more diplomatic, but I was outraged at the thought of him treating my mom that way. And when I'm outraged, I say things first and think about them later. (That's not a communication tip, by the way.)

"It's a little more complicated than that," Mom said, glancing in the rear-view mirror. "Sometimes, a person honestly doesn't know what they want."

"So what? He's still a jerk."

My text alert sounded again.

Lend a Hand meeting later. Can you make it?

So it *was* about that stupid club. Not that I was disappointed.

"Go ahead and answer your message," Mom said. "We have lots of time to talk."

I hesitated, trying to decide what to say.

I have plans with my mom.

"Done," I said to Mom. "So, are you okay?"
"I'm a little sad. But, yes, I'm okay."
"Well, he's a moron. And I never liked him."
That wasn't true. I'd thought Ray was nice, and fun, too. Fortunately, loyalty to my dad had kept me from ever saying so to anyone.

Mom just smiled. She probably saw through me, but if she did, she didn't call me on it. Instead, she changed the subject by asking if there was anything new with Dennis, which, coincidentally, was exactly when another message came through from him.

You doing anything tomorrow?

"He's the one texting me," I said. Then something came over me and I went ahead and told her about last weekend and how he'd told Stephanie about the dumb thing I'd done.

"I bet he doesn't see it the way you do," Mom said. "To him, it's probably just a funny story, while, to you, it's embarrassing. And maybe he doesn't know what this girl—Stephanie—is like. She might be showing a very different side to him."

That was true. If Dennis had seen what Stephanie was really like, he'd have hidden in the bushes when he saw her coming, instead of being friendly. I wasn't so sure about the rest of it, but it might not hurt to find out.

"He wants to know what I'm doing tomorrow," I said.

"Sounds like he's interested."

"Or he wants me to help him clean someone else's yard."

"That could still be a good sign," Mom said. "I'm sure there are lots of people he could ask."

"True." It *was* true! Dennis wouldn't have had any trouble finding someone else—if that was what he wanted. He might even have got someone who wouldn't empty an urn on the lawn. I decided to text him back, but I was careful not to sound too eager, interested or available.

Not sure. What's up?

I didn't have long to wait for his answer.

Nothing special. Just thought maybe we could hang out.

I might have squealed when I saw that. Just a little *eeek*, mind you—not like a horror movie, blood-curdling shriek or anything.

Unfortunately, Mom is one of those drivers who overreacts. She took my itty-bitty scream as a sure sign that we were about to run over a parade of baby strollers, or be hit by a rogue tank or something. The car jerked to a stop as she stomped on the brakes (good thing we were wearing seat belts) and yelled, *"What? What is it?"*

Behind us, tires squealed and a horn blasted. I looked over my shoulder in time to see a man in a truck shaking his fist. A second later he pulled out and around us. I won't bother describing the gesture he made driving past.

"Sorry about that," I said. "I got another text from Dennis."

"Well, that's all that matters." Mom patted her chest rapidly. "Don't worry about me. Really—I'm okay."

"Sorry," I repeated.

Mom gulped for air a couple of times. I think she might have been overdoing it a bit, but I didn't want to accuse her, so I used her tactic of changing the subject.

"Dennis wants me to hang out with him tomorrow. Is that okay?"

"Of course," she said. But I didn't miss the fact

that there'd been a slight hesitation, which was just enough to clear the cotton-candy Dennis haze from my head.

What had I been *thinking*? My mother had just been dumped by the only guy she'd dated since the divorce! And I was going to take off and leave her alone on one of the few days we had together. I had to be the worst daughter in the world.

"You know what? I think I'm going to play hard-to-get instead."

Mom smiled. "Never hurts to keep them guessing," she said.

So, I texted Dennis that I'd just remembered something else I had to do. I'd been dreaming about a moment like this for a long, long time, and it was hard to turn him down, but it was the right thing to do, and I knew it.

It also turned out to be a big mistake.

Huge.

Eighteen

"This is the shortest weekend we've ever had together."

It was true—Mom had been called in to work on Sunday afternoon, so she was dropping me back home after a little more than twenty-four hours at her place.

"I'll make up for it," she promised as she pulled into the driveway. "Maybe we can go somewhere special for supper on Wednesday, instead of eating in."

"Sure." I hugged her, grabbed my bag and stepped out of the car just as Dad appeared in the front doorway. He gave Mom a wave as she backed out.

"That wasn't much of a visit," he said as I neared the house. "I hope nothing is wrong."

"Nope. Everything's fine. Mom just had to

work." I kicked off my shoes inside the door and tossed my bag on the hall table.

"I wasn't expecting you so soon." He coughed and shuffled his feet.

I stopped mid-step in the hallway and turned my full attention on him. Was it my imagination or was he *nervous* about something?

"I mean, I thought you'd be gone until this evening—that's all."

"Is there some reason you don't want me here?"

"Of course not," he said with a weak laugh. "Don't want you here! What an idea."

He was *definitely* nervous, and I was getting more suspicious with every word that came out of his mouth. Besides, he kept glancing anxiously toward the kitchen doorway, as if he had something hidden in there.

Something—or some*one*!

It couldn't ... or could it be ... *Glenda*?

"I think I'll get a snack," I said. I spun around and hurried down the hall before Dad had a chance to stall me. As I burst into the kitchen I was more than ready to confront whoever was there.

Except there was nobody. That was confusing, considering the guilt that was all over my dad's face when he joined me a few seconds later.

"Why don't you sit down and let me make you something?" he said.

It isn't unusual for Dad to cook—we take turns in the kitchen—but it *was* strange for him to rush in there and offer to whip me up a snack. Like I suddenly need someone to spread peanut butter on a piece of bread, or spoon me up some yogurt or whatever.

"What would you like to have?"

How about an explanation for your strange behaviour?

"You know what? I'm not that hungry after all. I think I'll just grab a glass of milk."

"I'll get it!" Dad was at the fridge in a flash. He reached in, grabbed the milk jug and hurried to the cupboard for a glass, which he filled and put in front of me.

"Uh, thanks." *What* was he up to?

It came to me as he put the milk back, giving himself away by opening the fridge just enough to slip the jug inside. There was something in there that he didn't want me to see.

This was getting weirder by the minute, and there was no way I was leaving the kitchen without getting a look at whatever he was hiding. I drained the milk and took my glass to the sink.

"I guess I'll go put my stuff away." I sauntered toward the doorway.

Dad relaxed and took a few steps away from the fridge, which is when I spun around, rushed over and flung it open.

Nothing. At least, nothing out of the ordinary. He'd gotten a head start on dinner—steaks marinating and salads made—but that was about as interesting as it got.

"Uh ... Zoey?" Dad looked alarmed.

"I had an urge for a kiwi, but we're out." Hoping that would cover for my strange behaviour, I made a hasty exit.

I was in my room, halfway through a Biology assignment, when it finally occurred to me that Dad hadn't known I was going to be home for dinner when he got that stuff ready. The steaks and salads weren't for my dad and *me*—they were for my dad and *someone else*!

Glenda's sneaky face rose in my mind. Her overdone makeup and too-tight clothing, that eye-batting and all those fake smiles. How could a poor, lonely man like my father defend himself against that? I'd done my best to drive her off, but I could see I'd failed.

Even so, there was no way I was giving up!

I was planning my next strategy when there was a tap at my bedroom door.

"Can I come in?"

"Sure, Dad."

The door swung open and, after a slight hesitation, he crossed the room and sat on the edge of the bed. He cleared his throat a couple of times before speaking.

"There's something I want to mention."

"You're having someone over for dinner."

"I, er, yes, I am. How did you know?"

"I noticed you had dinner for two started," I said. I kept my voice casual, like it was no biggie.

"Of course, you're welcome to join us," he said, trying hard but failing miserably to look enthusiastic. He might as well have been holding up a sign that said "I'M LYING."

"Is it anyone I know?"

"Actually, it is. She and I have had a few, very casual dates. So casual that you could hardly even call them dates, really."

I wondered why he was avoiding her name. Maybe it hadn't occurred to him that I'd see who it was when she was chowing down in our dining room. It definitely hadn't occurred to him that my female instincts had already figured out the whole sordid business.

"It's someone from Therapy Solutions, isn't it?"

He looked startled. Then his face turned red.

"Uh, yes, but like I said, it's all been very casual so far."

This was the point where I might have

crossed a line ever so slightly. I shrugged, and said, "Whatever. But there was something else I wanted to talk to you about."

"Oh?"

"It's Mom. Did you know she's single again? She broke up with Ray."

"What? Are you sure?"

"Totally." Okay, so it hadn't happened quite the way I said. A minor technicality. She broke up with him—he broke up with her ... what difference did it really make? The part that mattered was that Mom was on her own again, and that much was true.

"Did she mention why?"

"Not really." I let that hang in the air, hoping he would think I knew more about it than I was free to say. Because if *anything* was going to stop him from seeing Glenda, it was the thought that he and Mom might get back together.

"I'm sure she had her reasons."

And he was dying to know what they were. I'd have to let Mom know I'd fibbed a bit about the breakup. Maybe I could persuade her to go along with it. After all, who wants to be known as the person who got dumped?

"Well, I didn't come in to grill you about your mother," Dad said, standing up. "I, uh, I'll let you get back to your homework now."

He didn't close the door behind him, and a moment later I heard him talking quietly on the phone. That nearly sent me into a panic—what if he'd called Mom right away? If so, I could only hope that he'd think I was confused.

But a moment later I found out I'd had nothing to worry about. I heard Dad end the call, and a second later he came back down the hall and stuck his head into my room again.

"Slight change of plans," he said. "I called my, uh, guest, and told her something came up."

I pictured Glenda, blotchy with anger (and too much makeup). It made me smile, until I noticed Dad frowning.

"Sorry," I told him. "I'm just happy that one of those steaks is mine now."

It was obvious he didn't buy that, but, as usual, his analysis of my reaction was way off.

"I hope you're not reading too much into this," he said. "We've all been through a lot, and I wouldn't want you to set yourself up for disappointment by hoping for something that will probably never happen."

I nodded thoughtfully, as though I could see the wisdom in what he'd just said (which actually sounded a lot like advice he should have been giving *himself*, but I didn't mention that) and told him, "Okay, thanks, Dad."

He smiled. "I'm always here if you need me, Zoey. Now, I'll let you get back to your school work."

I thought about how glad I was that I'd resisted the urge to text Dennis when Mom first got called in to work. I'd been *so* tempted to ask if he still wanted to hang out, but I hadn't wanted to look too eager. Now, as I got back to my Biology, it didn't seem like much of a sacrifice, considering that my dad and Glenda would have been enjoying a cozy dinner if I hadn't been here to prevent it.

I was feeling pretty good about that when Dad reappeared in the doorway. I couldn't read the odd expression on his face.

"Uh, could you come out here for a minute, Zoey?"

I pushed away from my desk and followed him. As we reached the front hall I saw that a police officer was standing there.

"So," Dad said, "here she is. Go ahead and ask her yourself."

The cop cleared his throat. "My name is Officer Caffrey, Miss Dalton, and I'm investigating a bit of an unusual occurrence on this street on Friday night. Do you know the Kimuras?"

My heart sank into my shoes. "Yes," I said.

In my peripheral vision, I saw Dad shaking his

head, as if he just couldn't believe his innocent daughter was being questioned by the police— and about something so silly.

"And are you aware that, the night before last, someone took all the leaves out of their yard?"

"Yes."

"Of course she is. I told her about it. Everyone on the block has heard about it by now," Dad said.

Officer Caffrey glanced at Dad and raised an eyebrow, but when he spoke again, it was to me.

"Did you have anything to do with the leaves being taken?"

I opened my mouth, then closed it again. I remembered the people who had passed by as Bean and I raked. Did any of them know me? What would happen if I just denied it? Were the police really going to push this thing?

I wondered if the Kimuras had pointed the finger at me, because of the whole newspaper fiasco. But, even if they had, that wasn't proof. Or maybe there was no real reason to suspect me. It was possible that the officer was asking everyone.

"Zoey?"

Dad's voice startled me, and I realized I'd been thinking so hard about what to say that I'd let a suspicious amount of time pass without answering.

A flash of clarity struck me and I knew that,

even if it meant I might get away with it, I just couldn't stand there and lie. I tried a different way out.

"Um, is it a crime to rake someone's yard ... *as a good deed*, Officer?"

Dad's mouth fell open.

"Then it *was* you?"

"Yes. But, like I said—"

"It was a good deed," Caffrey said, finishing my sentence. He didn't look impressed by my act of charity.

"Right."

"And was it a good deed when you stole their newspapers a few weeks ago?"

I tried to answer. I tried to explain. Except, everything came out garbled, as if I was talking through a mouthful of marbles. And the whole time, Dad kept staring like he'd never seen me before.

When it was clear, even to me, that everything I said was making it worse, I decided a new strategy was called for.

"I plead the Fifth."

Officer Caffrey covered a laugh by pretending to cough into his hand.

"The Fifth is an amendment to the U.S. Constitution," my dad said. "And that's only *one* of the reasons it doesn't apply."

"Then I want a lawyer," I mumbled. And I burst into tears.

As I fought to get the sobbing under control, I heard Dad talking to the officer.

"I think we can get to the bottom of this quickly if I could take the lead in asking questions. Would that be all right?"

Caffrey agreed, although he said he'd "reserve the right to jump in if necessary," and Dad ushered us into the living room. He wasted no time in getting started.

"The first thing I want you to know is that no one is judging you, Zoey."

Just as I'd feared. It was Therapy Dad.

Nineteen

Having a therapist for a parent is bad enough when things are going along smoothly, but when you mess up—watch out. I've wondered sometimes if my dad's main motivation in becoming a psychologist was to prepare himself for these moments. Never mind his patients, never mind his work at the hospital—I'm almost positive that analyzing me is what he *really* lives for.

I pulled myself together and tried to speed things up by calmly explaining the whole situation with the Kimuras—from the newspaper to the leaves. Unfortunately, full disclosure wasn't enough to stop Dad. He kept butting in with questions and comments and thoughtful nods. (I'll spare you the details of what he said, mainly because I wasn't actually listening.)

Officer Caffrey's eyes glazed over a few times

while this went on. I knew how he felt. Finally, he held up a hand and said, "I think it's clear what happened here, Miss Dalton, and I don't believe you meant any harm, but the fact is, you were still trespassing. I'll have a word with Mr. and Mrs. Kimura and, hopefully, they'll decide not to pursue this any further."

"You mean, I might still be in trouble, even though I was trying to be helpful?"

"Let's just wait and see what happens."

"I don't understand what they were upset about. I mean, I get how it looked with the newspapers, but why would they think someone raking their leaves was a bad thing?"

"Apparently, it's part of their lawn care system. They let the leaves stay on the ground until spring, and then they mow them into a kind of mulch to help fertilize the soil."

"What a great idea!" Dad said. Then he flushed with embarrassment, as though he'd done a terrible thing, commenting on a work-saving tip while his only child was being interrogated about her neighbourhood crime spree.

If Officer Caffrey was scandalized, he managed to hide it. He told us he'd be in touch shortly but not to worry in the meantime. Then he was gone.

I took a deep breath and waited for Dad to tell me he was disappointed that I hadn't felt I could trust him with all of this earlier. I didn't have to wait long, but he didn't say much else (to my surprise), and by the time we sat down to eat our steaks and salad, it seemed he'd forgotten all about it.

I decided he was too busy thinking about Mom and her new single status to care about a bunch of troublemaking leaves. And that was fine with me.

What *wasn't* fine was the way everything was going wrong with my random acts. For just a minute, I thought about giving up on the whole thing. But then I realized something. I'd just been questioned by the police—about a good deed! I figured that pretty much had to be hitting rock bottom when it came to random acts, which meant my luck was due to change for the better. It had to.

I really believed that.

I stopped believing it Monday morning, which started out on a slightly bad note that quickly got a whole lot worse.

I was on my way to homeroom when I sensed movement to my left—someone was trying to get my attention.

It was Destiny. She slowed as she reached my side and fell into the rhythm of my walk.

"Hey, Zoey."

"Hi, Destiny. What's up?"

"What's up is that you missed a super meeting on Saturday."

Before I had time to respond, Destiny rushed on. "We decided we're going to throw a special party just for members. *And* we're getting T-shirts printed." A proud smile lit up her face.

"Wow. You guys should record some of that and post it on YouTube to inspire others."

The smile was gone in a flash. Destiny's eyes narrowed. "What's that supposed to mean?" she demanded.

"Nothing. Never mind." Why even bother pointing out that her so-called good deed club hadn't actually been helping anyone? It seemed to be nothing more than a social group she was using to feed her own ego.

"To be honest, I've kind of lost interest," I said. "In the group, I mean. Not in helping people."

Her eyes narrowed. "Suit yourself," she snapped. Then she melted away into a crowd of middle-graders shuffling gloomily toward the start of a new week. I knew I'd just joined Bean on Destiny's list of people to revile, but the thought didn't bother me all that much.

I can't say the same for the second unpleasant encounter that morning. It happened between classes, when I passed Dennis talking to a couple of other guys outside a science lab.

"Oh, Zoey," he said, stepping away from the others. "I wanted to let you know that I gave Amanda those notes."

There was no smile on his face.

"What notes?" I asked uneasily.

"The ones that got wet. I guess you left them in our car that time we drove you home. Gary found them under the seat the other day. I went ahead and gave them to Amanda on Saturday."

I stood frozen in place, while my face twisted itself into some kind of demented grimace. Eventually, I managed to whisper, "Okay."

And then he was gone, without another word. Amanda Trecartin—the person who had vowed to track down whoever was responsible for the nasty quiz about Destiny—had just been handed the one piece of evidence she needed.

And Dennis. He hadn't said so, but I knew one hundred percent that he'd figured it out.

All of his former friendliness was gone—along with whatever might or might not have been happening between us.

I made up my mind that I was *not* going think about that. It was over and that was that. Besides, I had more immediate things to worry about.

The rest of the morning was a blur of worry and panic. Over and over I pictured Amanda looking at my notes and realizing there was something familiar about the handwriting. How long would it be before it clicked? I knew it hadn't happened yet or I'd have heard about it, but it was only a matter of time.

I had to do something.

As I went through my options, it became clear that there was only one sensible solution. I had to sneak into Amanda's house and ransack the place until I found those notes. (Yes, this actually seemed like my best plan for a while.) That was followed by a few other ideas that were, sadly enough, even less promising.

Eventually, I grasped the terrible truth. There was no way out. As soon as I was exposed, I would become a pariah, shunned by everyone. I'd have to quit school, or transfer to one far, far away. Maybe I could go live in Montreal with my mom's brother Serge and his wife, Penny. He has a serious foot odour problem, but even spending years in a house that smells like dirty socks sounded better than being a social outcast.

Or—maybe I could talk my dad into letting me switch to home-schooling. I imagined myself standing alone in my living room, wearing a grad gown and clutching a diploma I'd printed off the computer, while Dad clapped and smiled and insisted he was proud of me.

The gloom hadn't lifted by noon when I got to the cafeteria and sat down at our usual table. Bean and Mariska were already there, and before I could even open my mouth she leaned forward.

"Bean told me about it," she whispered. Then, no kidding, she winked.

"About *it*?" I should have known what she meant, but my head was too full of my new problems to process anything else at that moment.

Mariska did her best imitation of a silent movie clip next. She mouthed, "*The Random Act,*" in exaggerated slow motion. At the same time, she seemed to be trying to shove her eyebrows up to meet her hairline. When that was (thankfully) over, she put a finger to her lips and went, "Shhhhhhhh."

"Yeah, we're *real* proud of that," I snapped, annoyed at being reminded of the leaves while I was in the middle of a new crisis.

Mariska's smile dropped away and she drew back as if I'd slapped her.

"Hey!" Bean said.

I levelled a warning look at him. "It turns out there was a problem," I said. "A big one. But right now, I have other things on my mind, and I don't want to talk about that—or anything else."

When I glanced back at Mariska, I saw that her lower lip was trembling and her head was bent forward. She let out a pathetic mewling sound, like there was an injured kitten down her shirt. She followed that up by starting to hiccup.

Bean's arm snaked protectively around her shoulders, but his eyes never left my face. "What is *wrong* with you?" he demanded.

"She doesn't like me." Mariska sniffed. "I don't know why."

"She never gave you a chance," Bean said.

I knew instantly how this was going to end. If I didn't say something to make it better, Bean and Mariska were going to stomp off, and it could take days, or even weeks, to get things back to normal. I thought fast.

"That's not true," I told them. "I swear, I've honestly been *trying* to be nice to her! It was even one of my random acts."

It was the kind of thing that you keep hearing over and over after you've said it. One of those internal echoes that sounds increasingly like something only a complete moron would say.

I could tell I wasn't the only one with this particular loop playing in my head. Bean finally broke the silence.

"Being nice to *my girlfriend* was one of your random acts."

His voice was clipped and flat, which meant he was furious and trying hard to control himself. Not for my sake, of course—he just didn't want to blow up in front of Mariska.

"What's going on?" Jenna slid into the spot beside me, frowning and looking back and forth at what was clearly a hostile situation.

Bean told her what I'd said.

"Come on, Bean—you know she had to be kidding."

All eyes swung around to me. I squirmed a little—something I seemed to be doing a lot these days.

"I, uh, actually, I was trying to think of something to say to smooth things over, and that came out. Sorry, Mariska."

Bean's a guy, so he reacted like one. He rolled his eyes, shook his head, told me I was a dork and let it go. For him, that was the end of it. He went ahead and plowed into his lunch as if nothing had happened.

Mariska handled it a little differently. A little less forgivingly. She could have milked the whole thing for a lot more sympathy and attention, but I didn't get the sense she was upset because she'd been robbed of that chance. Looking at her, it seemed she genuinely felt hurt. I couldn't meet her eyes—the sadness in them was like an accusation.

It was pretty clear that I hadn't been doing a great job of being nice to her. Another random act fail.

"Mariska," I told her, "I really am sorry for hurting your feelings. I don't know what's wrong with me sometimes."

Then Jenna rolled her eyes and said, "That's just Zoey—she says the craziest things. It gets kind of annoying sometimes, but now that you're one of us I'm afraid you'll have to get used to it."

Now *that* was the perfect thing to say. Feeling accepted and part of the group was the one (and probably only) thing that could have made Mariska feel better.

She gave me a forgiving smile, and even reached her hand over and let it rest on mine for a second.

After lunch, as Jenna and I walked to our lockers, I thanked her for bailing me out, and added, "I don't know what was dumber—making that one of my random acts, or telling them about it."

"Telling them—obviously." She leaned closer and lowered her voice. "Being nice to Mariska was one of *my* random acts, too."

Twenty

I could not believe my eyes when Glenda walked into Therapy Solutions on Tuesday evening. If anything, she had cranked up the skank-wear, slinking into the waiting room in tight jeans and high heels. When she turned from hanging her jacket, I saw that she had on a flimsy blouse that, if you want my opinion, she hadn't quite finished buttoning up.

The second she sat down, her eyes shifted to my desk and she gave me a pitying smile. Heat rushed to my face. Her meaning couldn't have been any clearer if she'd walked over and told me straight up that I was wasting my time fighting her. She was not giving up, and she was definitely not planning to lose.

We'll see about *that*, I thought, as I levelled a steely smile right back at her. I hoped she could see that I wasn't intimidated. Whether or not she got my message I don't know, because Chantal came hurrying in and the attention in the room shifted as everyone waited for her sob-fest. She burst into tears right on cue and Glenda dug into her bag for a Kleenex and crossed the room to give it to her.

Mrs. Wilmox leaned past Sonny to tell Chantal, "You know, dear, if you would take my advice and pick up some B complex, I'm sure it would help."

Chantal blubbered on.

"I keep telling her to try vitamin B," Mrs. Wilmox said to Sonny, who was on her left, "but she won't listen."

Sonny glanced up from his phone and nodded, which could have meant anything but more than likely meant nothing. He rarely speaks in the waiting room, probably because of his stutter. I don't know what he's like in session, which the buzzer on my desk signified was about to begin.

As always, the group stood as soon as they heard it, making Dad's instruction to "send them in" unnecessary. They filed through the doorway, passing him on their way. He greets each of them every session.

"Good to see you, Chantal. Good evening, Sonny. Hello, Karla."

I watched carefully as Glenda reached him. She barely nodded, and her voice was inaudible when she answered his greeting. A shadow crossed his face—there and gone so quickly that I would have missed it if I hadn't been watching like a hawk.

I thought about the odd exchange while group was in session. Obviously, she was up to something, acting cold and withdrawn instead of being her usual flirty self.

It didn't take me long to figure out her new game. She was angry that he'd cancelled their dinner on Sunday. Her muttered greeting and refusal to smile were to let him know she wasn't happy about it. The way she was dressed, that could only be to show him what he was missing. It was a carefully calculated plan, and I couldn't help worrying that it was going to work.

I knew I could put another note on her windshield, but my heart wasn't in it. Besides, my dad had already admitted that they'd had a few dates. That proved how well my note-writing plan had worked. As in, not at all.

I wished I could see into the therapy room so I could get a look at what she was up to. Sure, she went in there pouting, but that was probably just so she could draw him in. She'd have switched back to flirting by now.

Too bad the keyhole on the deadbolt was impossible to see through. (Don't ask how I know that—I've already embarrassed myself enough for one week.) But as I stared gloomily at the door, I realized there *was* a way to see past it—at the bottom. Between the floor and the lower edge of the door there was a space of about half an inch.

Session had started less than five minutes ago—there was no way anyone would have a reason to open the door. I crossed over to it and dropped to my knees before I could talk myself out of it. Kneeling forward wasn't enough, though—I couldn't get close enough to the floor to see into the room. I flattened out on my stomach, pressed the left side of my face firmly into the carpet and closed my right eye. Better, but not great. I could sort of see shoes, and the bottoms of the chair legs. Nothing was clear, and the most I could tell was that they were seated in a circle.

I squinted, trying to make out Glenda's high-heeled shoes, which was when I heard something I wasn't expecting—the sound of the waiting-room door opening and someone coming in.

I gasped, choked a bit on a piece of lint I'd inhaled off the floor, and then sat up and turned to see who it was.

Bill! How could I have forgotten that his job makes him a few minutes late now and then? Or not realized he wasn't with the others? (I have no choice but to blame him for that—if he wasn't so quiet all the time, it wouldn't be so easy to overlook him.)

He stood there, blinking, like he was waking up from a deep sleep.

"Oh, hi, Bill." I got to my feet. "I guess you're wondering what I was doing."

Bill's eyebrows went up. He didn't speak.

"I, uh, I dropped something."

The eyebrows dove toward each other in an instant frown. It was the frown of someone whose intelligence has been insulted.

"What did you drop?"

If I hadn't panicked, I might have said a pen. A paperclip. A thumbtack. But I blurted out the first thing that came into my head, which was, "The stapler."

"The stapler," he echoed. His eyebrows shot back up. I wished they'd pick a position and stick to it. "Do you think it rolled under the door?"

"No, uh, I was—"

"Spying?"

"Really, it's not what you think," I said.

"What I *think* … is that your father needs to

know what you do when group is in session." He took a few steps toward the session room.

"No! Please! I swear, I've never done that before."

Bill hesitated, and I could see that he was thinking about what to do. Even though he was outraged, his natural tendency to avoid attention made him willing to be persuaded.

"I wasn't snooping," I insisted. And then, in desperation, I decided that the only thing I could do was come clean. If Bill knew why I was flat on the floor with my eyeball squashed against the door, maybe he'd be more understanding.

"I just wanted to see what Glenda was doing," I explained. I lowered my voice and whispered, "She's been after my father and I don't think it's right, what with him being her doctor and everything."

"Glenda has been after—your father?" Bill seemed more shocked by this than he'd been over my spying. I took that as a hopeful sign.

"That's right," I said. "They've even had a few dates."

"Glenda and Dr. Dalton have been *dating?*"

It occurred to me too late that if Bill had been prepared to turn *me* in over a little spying, he was just as likely to confront my dad over something like this. Fortunately, he did neither. What he *did* do was turn around without another word and walk back out the door.

A reprieve—but I knew it was temporary. My dad would have Miss Barducci call Bill tomorrow to see why he'd been a no-show— and I'd be busted. I decided to see if I could catch him and talk him into coming back inside. Or, at the very least, get him to promise that he wouldn't tell anyone what I'd just told him.

Grabbing my jacket, I tugged it on as I pounded down the stairs and out the door that opened onto the parking lot. Bill had already crossed to where the cars were parked. I called his name as he lifted his arm and aimed his keychain at one of the cars.

The brake lights lit up as he reached the driver's door and pulled it open. I called again but, if he heard me, he didn't answer. Seconds later the car was backing up and I watched helplessly as it shifted into drive and moved past me and out onto the street.

It had almost reached the corner before I realized the most peculiar thing. Bill had just taken off in Glenda's car!

Twenty-One

Two or three minutes must have passed while I stood there trying to make sense of what I'd just seen. Bill didn't *seem* like a car thief, and yet I'd just caught him in the act. Could it be that what I'd just told him had made him furious enough to lash out at Glenda—thinking her actions could jeopardize the entire group?

I also wondered how he'd managed to get Glenda's keys without me noticing—until I remembered the time he'd put on her jacket by mistake. Maybe she kept a spare in one of her pockets, and he'd taken it.

The sooner the police were alerted to the theft, the sooner they'd catch him, so I knew I had to report it. But Dad was going to wonder what I'd been doing in the parking lot. How would I explain that?

There wasn't much time to sort it all out before I got back upstairs. I did the best I could, and by the time I tapped on the session room door, I was ready.

The murmur of voices stopped immediately, and a moment later the door opened a few inches. Dad's face appeared.

"Zoey? Is something wrong?"

"Uh, kind of. It's Bill. He was just here—but he was acting strange and then he ran out. I was worried, so I followed him downstairs and—he stole Glenda's car."

"Bill stole Glenda's car?"

"Yes. I saw him drive away in it."

The door opened more and Glenda came into view. "Did you just say something about my car?"

I repeated what I'd said to Dad.

"You're sure it was my car?" Glenda asked.

"Positive." Glenda had the only red car in the group, and the back fender on the driver's side had a scrape in it. That was definitely the car I'd seen Bill driving.

"Was it a black SUV?" Glenda prodded.

"What?" I decided she was describing Bill's car, hoping I was mixed up. "No, it was your car—the red one."

"Oh," Glenda said. Then she laughed, which wasn't quite the reaction I'd been expecting.

"Should I call the police?" I asked.

"No, you shouldn't. That's *Bill's* car."

"But I saw you driving it!" I insisted.

"You probably did," she agreed. "A few months ago my SUV was in for repairs and Bill let me borrow his car a couple of times."

"Well, good then. So that's settled," Dad said. He turned to Glenda. "Could you excuse me for a moment? I need to speak to Zoey. Tell the others I'll be right there."

Glenda nodded and returned to her seat while Dad stepped into the reception area and tugged the door shut behind him.

"You said that Bill was behaving strangely?" I couldn't tell from his face if he was worried or confused or both.

"Yeah. But I could have imagined that."

"But he was here? And then he ran out?"

"Yeah—that's what I thought was strange. But he probably just remembered something he had to do."

It was easy to see that Dad was still concerned, but with his group waiting for him in the next room he let it go. For now.

My knees had gone weak. As the session

room door closed behind Dad, I made my way unsteadily back behind the desk and collapsed into the chair. My head and heart were having a competition to see which one could race the fastest.

What a mess.

"This cannot get any worse," I muttered to myself, which was the precise second that I realized it *could*.

On top of everything, the significance of something else became suddenly, horrifyingly clear. I'd been putting the notes intended for Glenda on the wrong car. Specifically, I'd been putting them on Bill's car. Which could mean only one thing.

I was Bill's stalker!

I didn't get much sleep that night. I'd start to drift off, but my brain kept reminding me of all the things that had gone wrong in the last few days. The Kimuras' leaves. The meeting notes that Dennis had handed over to Amanda (and the end of any hope that Dennis and I might become a couple). The things I'd told Bill. The secret admirer messages I'd left on what had turned out to be Bill's car. It was like a pack of random act wolves circling me, each waiting their chance to pounce.

It wasn't fair! My intentions had been good, hadn't they? Most of them, anyway. Okay, if I was completely honest about it, the notes I'd been writing to Glenda were meant to get rid of her—but don't forget that they could *also* have made her feel special. Plus, if she'd actually gotten them, and they'd worked, it would have been a good deed for my dad.

I wondered what Dad was going to say when he found out I'd spied on the group and told Bill about his dates with Glenda. He didn't ground me very often but I had a feeling this would be one of those times.

School the next day was a nightmare. I couldn't concentrate for worrying about what I might be in for when I got home, and, of course, about Amanda figuring out the handwriting thing and exposing me as the person who wrote the quiz. Every time I glimpsed her, my stomach clenched and it got hard to breathe. Then I had an idea.

After school I hurried to her locker. She was cramming books into it, though I don't quite know how. The inside was packed nearly solid with clothes and bags and all kinds of stuff.

"Hey, Amanda," I said, keeping my voice casual.

"Put your foot on this for a sec," she said, pointing to an overstuffed gym bag in the bottom of her locker.

I did as she asked, yanking my foot back as she forced the door shut.

"Thanks." She turned toward me. "Did you want something?"

"Um, yeah. Dennis told me he gave you my notes from that meeting and I was feeling a bit guilty."

"Yeah? About what?"

"The thing is, I couldn't find them when I typed up the report for you, so I kind of did it by memory. I could fix the report so it's accurate if you give them back to me."

"Sorry, can't do it."

Was it my imagination, or was she avoiding looking at me? Prickles of sweat made me start to itch all over. I tried, unsuccessfully, to keep my voice from shaking as I asked, "Why not?"

Amanda took a deep breath and finally made eye contact. "I threw them out, that's why. I threw out everything to do with that stupid club."

"So, they're gone?"

"Afraid so."

"It's okay," I said. I somehow kept myself from

hugging her, which might have seemed odd. "So, did something happen with the group, or did you just get bored?"

"I got tired of being *used*," she snapped, like it was my fault.

"You mean, for good deeds?"

"Good deeds," she sneered. "As if. *I* was supposed to be part of the Leadership Team, not some grubby do-gooder. But Destiny treated me like I was her errand girl."

I shook my head as if I sympathized, which I definitely did *not*. It wasn't that I was exactly shocked that some group members never actually intended to help anyone—it was just strange to hear her admit it that openly.

My steps felt a little lighter the rest of the afternoon, even though I still had to face Dad. He'd ground me, or tell me he was disappointed in me, or both, but a little grounding was nothing compared to the thought of being a social outcast at school.

And then, the day got even better. I got a text from Mom reminding me that we were going out for dinner, which might even mean I'd be able to avoid Dad until tomorrow. That would give him time to cool off, in which case he could (fingers crossed) decide to let the whole thing slide. Assuming he'd even talked to Bill. There was always a chance, however small, that Bill would take pity and not rat me out.

As soon as I got home from school I wrote a note reminding Dad about my plans with Mom. It wasn't likely he'd have forgotten, but I figured the note made me look responsible. I needed to line up all the pluses I could.

Mom swung by right after work and I was out the door and into her car in a flash. Dad would be getting home any minute and it was all I could do not to yell "Go! Go! Go!" like someone trying to escape a crazed killer in a movie. She took her time backing out of the driveway, but when we headed in the opposite direction from where Dad would be coming I knew I was in the clear—for the time being.

"Where are we going to eat?" I asked.

"I'm kind of in the mood for Italian—how about Mrs. Novielli's?"

"Sure!"

The place was already filling up when we got there but we were lucky enough to get a table right away. When our waiter arrived Mom ordered Pollo Toscanini and I went for a Marinara pizza. Mom asked for ice water with lemon for both of us. She has a theory that it makes your food taste better.

While we waited for our food, Mom asked me if there was anything new with Dennis.

"I think he might have liked me, but things got messed up."

"In what way?"

"Well, there was Stephanie the Psycho," I said slowly. "And other things. A misunderstanding, really, but I don't want to get into it."

"I see," Mom said. "Well, try not to be discouraged. And mostly, don't dwell on it."

"Okay. Thanks, Mom," I said. Not because I thought it was particularly great advice (what would *she* know about the teen dating scene?) but because I could tell she really wanted to help. And I knew she must still feel bad about Ray dumping her for his ex.

I was about to ask how she was doing with the breakup when our food arrived. My pizza toppings were still sizzling and the smell of the garlic and basil and tomato made my mouth water. Mom's chicken and pasta looked good, too, and for a moment we were silent as we dug into our meals.

I polished off my first slice of pizza and then went ahead and asked, "So, is there anything new or different since the weekend? With Ray, I mean."

"You mean since I broke up with him?"

Uh-oh.

I'd completely forgotten to talk to her about what I'd told Dad. (Who could blame me with everything else that was going on?) I put my fork down and took a deep breath.

"I guess you were talking to Dad."

"Yes, I was. And you can imagine how surprised I was to hear the interesting version of the breakup that he'd been told."

"I was just trying to help him."

"Help him?" Mom looked me square in the eye. "You know very well that your father has had a difficult time since the end of our marriage. Do you think it's helpful to put false ideas in his head?"

"I wasn't looking at it that way," I admitted. "He was making a mistake, and it was the first thing I could think of to stop him."

"What kind of mistake?"

"Dating the wrong person," I told her glumly.

"Who your father dates is his business," Mom said, but I could see she was surprised to hear he was dating anyone.

"Okay, but—"

"But nothing. Your father is an adult. It is *not* your place to be running interference in his life."

"Fine." I tried to look penitent. "Are you going to tell Dad?"

"No, I'm not."

I was breathing a small sigh of relief when she added, "*You* are."

Twenty-Two

I texted both Jenna and Bean the second I had a chance. Not that I expected much help from Jenna—she's almost never in any kind of trouble at home. Bean, on the other hand, practically lives in tight spots. If anyone could think of a way for me to squirm out of the sticky situation I was in, it would be him.

Jenna got back to me in a matter of seconds. And, just as I thought, she was no help at all.

Bean was no help either, but for a different reason. He was at Mariska's house, playing some stupid board game with her and her parents.

As I set my phone down I realized what had been bothering me about Mariska. It wasn't actually *her*. Sure, she had her annoying moments, but not annoying enough to make me feel this ... whatever it was I felt toward her.

That was because of what had been happening to Bean since they'd started going out.

It sounds cliché to say it was like I'd lost my best friend, but that was true. Bean was my go-to guy, the one I talked to about everything. Now? If I needed him, chances were good that he'd be busy (like now). And there was also a chance (like a hundred percent) that anything I told him was going to be passed on to Mariska. Which is stupid, but it's the way things go sometimes.

I knew I still had Jenna, except it wasn't the same with her. Bean knows how to listen and not say anything. Jenna never does that. She gives advice. Lots of it. And every bit is solid and sensible and a complete pain in the butt. So, I'm careful about the things I tell her, which I never had to be with Bean—until Mariska.

It's strange that I was thinking about all of this while I was walking to school on Thursday morning, and then, when I got there, I found Mariska in the hallway near my locker. And what was she doing? Defending me—to Stephanie Roth!

Up until that moment, I'd mostly seen the people-pleaser side of Mariska. I've got to say, the nasty side was a whole lot more interesting.

"Do you even *know* how pathetic you look, going around threatening people to stay away from Dennis Fuller?" Mariska was practically shouting, and she kept stepping closer and closer to Stephanie, until I thought their noses would touch.

"Shut up," Stephanie muttered, inching backward.

"No, *you* shut up! Shut up talking trash about my friend. And shut up bossing people around. You're not in charge of who Dennis Fuller talks to!"

Stephanie's face had turned a deep red, which was no wonder. A crowd had gathered with the usual school hallway speed, and everyone could hear what Mariska was saying. That meant the entire student body would know all about it before the day was over—including Dennis.

Stephanie's mouth opened and closed a few times but nothing came out. She spun around and practically bolted down the hall. Mariska watched until she was out of sight.

"Wow," I said as I reached her side. "What was that about?"

Mariska shrugged. "Stephanie thought it was okay to put down one of my friends. She knows better now."

By the looks on the nearby faces and the buzz in the hallway, it was safe to say the whole school knew better.

"Wow. I've never had anyone stand up for me like that before," I said. "Thank you *so* much."

Mariska waved away my thanks, as if a good throw-down was her favourite way to start the day. But I could see she was pleased all the same.

"Remind me to stay on your good side, Mariska," Jenna said from behind me. I swung around to face her.

"How much of that did you catch?" I asked.

"All of it—I was just over there," she said, nodding vaguely to her left. "It was wild!"

"I know! I could hardly believe what I was seeing," I said.

Mariska grinned at us. "I'm small but mighty."

And *loyal*, I thought in a flush of silent shame. That was more than I could say about how I'd treated her, and I promised myself I would be a good, solid friend to her from that moment on. I smiled at her, and it was probably the first one-hundred-percent genuine one she ever got from me.

The crowd was melting away now that the show was over, and Jenna and I opened our lockers so we could get our things for first class, a task that took me about ten seconds. Not Jenna. She takes forever because, naturally, everything has to be organized and neat. So, Mariska and I were standing there talking, waiting for her, when Jenna said, "Oh, no!" and our attention shifted to her.

"You having some kind of Post-it Note emergency or something?" I asked.

Jenna looked around and lowered her voice, which told me this had something to do with a random act. Not my favourite subject at the moment.

"I brought cookies again, but the bag got ripped," she said. She pointed into her schoolbag, but since I don't have x-ray vision I had to take her word for it that there were cookies inside.

"Who are they for?" Mariska asked.

"The teachers. It's one of my—you know ..."

Random acts, Mariska mouthed silently.

"Exactly. I was going to sneak them into the teachers' lounge right after first class started, and then get a late pass. But I can't take them like this."

"Isn't that the container you used the last time?" I asked, pointing to the upper shelf in her locker. "The one you nearly lost your mind about getting back because your mom needed it so desperately?"

Jenna followed the direction of my finger. "I keep forgetting to take it home," she admitted. "But it's not washed out or anything."

"So what? It's cookie crumbs. Brush them out and it'll be good to go."

Mariska tugged the container off the shelf, snapped off the lid and looked it over. A sly smile crossed her face, and in a lightning-fast movement, her hand dipped inside the front of her shirt and came out with a tissue, which she used to dust out the inside of the container.

"It's fine," she said. "Just use it."

The warning bell rang then, so Mariska and I headed off to our morning classes, leaving Jenna alone to carry out her random act. After the disaster we'd had the first time she snuck cookies into the teachers' lounge, I crossed my fingers that she wouldn't run into any trouble.

I'd begun to think that our whole random acts thing was jinxed, but when we met for lunch Jenna told us everything had gone smoothly.

"I wasn't even nervous," she said. "In and out—though I did stop to count the microwaves. It's crazy how many they have in there."

"Yeah, I noticed that when I got your plastic dish the other week," Bean said. "How many are there?"

"Seven."

"Weird," Bean said.

Sadly, that was about the most interesting topic of conversation at our table during lunch.

The rest of the day passed by uneventfully, although it was a bit longer than usual because I had peer-tutoring after school. (Thanks a lot, whoever invented algebra.) My tutor, Sarah, is usually good for about half an hour. Then her eyes glaze over from the hopelessness of trying to get through to me. That's when she forces a super-bright smile onto her face and says, "Okay, well, I think you're starting to catch on. Do some review and we'll pick up here next time."

I was on my way home afterward when I remembered I hadn't faced the music there yet. I'd managed to avoid Dad the night before by dashing to my room with the claim of "tons of homework" after Mom dropped me off. (In this kind of emergency, education is my best shield against Dad's prodding and analyzing.) I still didn't know whether or not Dad had talked to Bill.

He wasn't home when I got there. I dropped my stuff in the hall and hurried to the kitchen to start dinner. I put some breaded fish fillets and fries in the oven, opened a can of peas, then set the table.

Dad arrived about fifteen minutes later. He

found me doing homework on the kitchen island. If he was upset with me, he sure didn't show it. He crossed the room, gave me a one-armed hug and sniffed the air.

"Do I smell dinner cooking?"

"Yes—it's in the oven."

"Excellent. How long before it's done?"

"Another ten minutes."

Dad glanced at his watch and headed down the hall to his office while I did a silent fist pump. Bill must have decided not to rat me out.

It looked like my luck might have changed for the better. Even with the way things had gone earlier, the day hadn't been all bad.

Of course, it wasn't over yet.

Twenty-Three

I'd been hoping Bill would give me some kind of signal when he got to Therapy Solutions on Thursday—something that would let me know everything was cool. That didn't happen, but he didn't act any different than other nights, and when he passed my desk and I said, "Hi, Bill," he answered me in his normal, shy way.

I took that as a good sign. And, anyway, what had I expected him to do? It's not like he could jump up and say, "By the way, Zoey, I'm not going to tell anyone that I found you with your face mashed on the floor, trying to see into the session room on Tuesday."

The week had been full of narrow escapes, but it seemed I was pretty much in the clear, and it felt awesome to relax.

I hadn't forgotten that I still had to tell Dad

I'd fibbed about Mom and Ray's breakup, but that was no biggie. If I acted like I'd meant to save Mom from the embarrassment of him knowing she got dumped, Dad would go easy on me. There might be a bit of a lecture, but that would be all.

I wished I could explain about the stalker business to Bill and put his mind at ease, but that was out of the question. I convinced myself that as time passed by without any more notes he'd relax and forget all about it. It was a relief to let myself off that hook!

I celebrated by helping myself to a couple of mints from Miss Barducci's secret stash. The sugar put me in a good mood and gave me a burst of energy so I did some dusting and tidied up the desk drawers. Then I browsed the app store on my phone. I was checking out dramatic music sounds when Dennis called.

It's amazing how many thoughts can race through a person's head in the time it takes for a phone to ring. I ignored the jumble in my brain and tried to calm my heart as I answered.

"Hello?"

"Hi, Zoey."

"Hey, Dennis."

Long seconds ticked by before he spoke again.

"Here's the thing. I might have made a mistake. So, I'm calling to ask you straight up. The quiz with all those nasty things about Destiny—*is* that *your* handwriting?"

My heart sank about as low as a heart can sink. I'm talking subterranean.

It was tempting to deny it, to remind him that he himself had said how lots of people write alike. To add another bit of deceit to the growing pile. Except, I knew I couldn't.

"Yes," I said. "But I—"

Dennis cut me off before I could explain how Bean and Jenna and I had just been messing around, or that we'd never meant for anyone else to see it.

"Thanks for being honest, at least," he said. There was another second or two of silence, and then he said goodbye.

There was a strangely hollow feeling inside me as I put my phone down. Of all the things that had gotten messed up lately, the quiz getting out hadn't even been my fault, but I was sure the one paying for it.

I reminded myself that Dennis was just one guy—it's not like there was a shortage. Besides, we'd never been anything more than casual friends. It should have been the easiest thing in the world to forget about him.

Except it wasn't. It hurt.

Lost in unhappy thoughts, I didn't pay any particular attention as the clients came out of the therapy room, got their jackets and left. And then, my father's voice broke in.

"Zoey?"

"Yeah, Dad?"

"Would you come in here for a moment?"

The tone of his voice told me there was trouble. Had Bill blabbed after all? The fear that he had made my legs a bit rubbery as I got up and crossed to the doorway where Dad was standing.

He stepped back to let me in, which was when I saw that both Bill and Glenda were still inside. The sight did not cheer me.

"Please sit down," Dad said. I did, and he added, "Bill asked to have you and Glenda present. Apparently, whatever it is he wants to discuss involves both of you."

I wondered if I might be able to make myself faint by holding my breath—but there was no time to find out. Bill started right in, explaining how he'd caught me trying to peek under the door on Tuesday.

To say Dad looked shocked would be an understatement. If I hadn't been in so much trouble, it might even have been amusing to see the calm, cool, professional expression disappear. His mouth dropped open and a red flush crept up his neck and onto his face.

"You're certain she was spying?" he asked when he'd recovered enough to speak.

"Well, she *said* she dropped the stapler," Bill answered, "but the stapler was sitting right there on the desk."

Stupid stapler.

Bill gave me a quick, sympathetic glance, like he was sorry for what he was doing. That didn't stop him from going on.

"I told Zoey I was going to have to let you know what I'd seen. That's when she tried to talk me out of it by explaining *why* she was trying to see under the door."

It was Dad's turn to look in my direction. I avoided meeting his eyes as Bill continued ratting me out.

"Zoey told me she was trying to see what Glenda was up to."

"*Glenda?*" Dad repeated. Glenda didn't react at all, which made me think she'd already heard the whole story. She was mostly focused on the floor, although she darted a look at me then.

"That's right. She said that Glenda has been 'after you.' It seems that made Zoey think she needed to keep an eye on the situation."

"*After* me? That's ridiculous," Dad said.

"Of course it's ridiculous," Glenda agreed, shaking her head.

"I'm afraid there's more." Bill sighed. "Zoey also claimed that you and Glenda have been dating."

My dad shot to his feet. "*What?* That's *outra-geous!*" For just a second, he grabbed the sides of his head with both hands, like it might otherwise roll right off his shoulders. When he turned to me, his eyes were wild and his voice was shaking.

"What the blazes is going on, young lady?"

I could hardly believe the performance I was seeing. Dating a patient might not have been ethical, but my father was no liar. Yet, here he was, denying it and acting shocked.

"But you told me that!" I reminded him, choking on the emotion of the moment.

"*I* told you I was dating Glenda?" he echoed.

I tried to remember his exact words. "Well, you didn't say Glenda, exactly, but you *did* say you were seeing someone from work—and I already knew she'd been after you. For the last few months she's been coming to therapy all dolled up."

"And that could only be because I was after your father?" Glenda asked, speaking for the first time.

"You were for sure after *someone!*" I said. "Who else could it be?"

Bill smiled.

Glenda smiled at Bill.

Oh.

Dad sank back onto his chair. A minute ticked by without anyone speaking. I was trying to put together something to say that might make this better but I didn't have a chance before Dad spoke.

"You two are in a relationship?"

Bill and Glenda nodded. She said, "We have been for a few months, actually."

"We should have told you," Bill added. "But we both liked the group and we knew one of us would have to leave it."

"It's a standard rule in group therapy," Dad said. "But we can talk about that another time."

"Actually," Glenda spoke up, "we've both decided to leave the group."

Dad frowned slightly. "Oh?"

Glenda glanced at Bill, who gave her a nod of encouragement. She took a deep breath and said, "We know what Zoey did was wrong, but, frankly, I don't believe she should take all the blame by herself. I think her actions were more a cry for help than anything else."

"A cry for help?"

"Yes, Doctor. A cry for help. You see, Zoey has shared a few things with me recently and, I have to tell you, I'm shocked at what goes on in your home."

For a split second I wondered what she was talking about. When it hit me, I thought I might faint without even needing to hold my breath.

Dad's frown deepened as Glenda went on.

"Zoey is *clearly* a desperately unhappy young woman, and it's no wonder with the things she's exposed to. A father who parades woman after woman through her life! Parenting so slack that she's allowed to date a musician-wannabe dropout who's in his late teens! And a man who tells his own daughter that he can't stand children!"

This last one choked her up so much that she couldn't go on. Bill reached over and patted her hand while my father sat as motionless as a stone.

"But none of those things were true!" I blurted. "I made them up so you'd lose interest in him. That is, when I thought you were after him."

Glenda blinked. "So, you aren't dating someone called Sloth?" she asked.

"Of course not. The stories and notes and everything—it was all just to keep you from dating my dad."

"Am I that awful?" Glenda asked softly.

"It wasn't like that," I said. "But you have a bunch of kids and—"

I stopped there, before I could make it worse (if that was possible), and that gave Bill a chance to speak again.

"What notes?" His eyes seemed to bore right into me. "You said the stories and *notes*."

Glenda put it together before I could untie my tongue. "She thought it was *my* car, Bill. The notes she put on your car were meant for me. And the one that was in your coat pocket—I'm guessing she got the jackets mixed up. We've done that ourselves."

Everyone turned to look at me again.

I said, "That's exactly right. I thought you might forget about my dad if you thought you had a secret admirer. I had no idea Bill was getting the notes, or that they'd cause the trouble they did."

"I see," Bill said, frowning.

"It seems the things we've blamed on Dr. Dalton have actually all been Zoey's fault," Glenda said. (I personally thought that point had already been made.)

Then Bill stood up, crossed over to my father and shook his hand. "I'm sorry about that, Dr. Dalton. It seems we jumped the gun a bit. I'll certainly want to continue seeing you, and I'm guessing Glenda will too."

Behind him, Glenda murmured her

agreement. She also dabbed the corners of her eyes with a tissue, which was when I realized she'd been blinking back tears.

Dad spoke then. "I'm glad you're willing to continue your therapy here, Bill, but *you* certainly don't have anything to apologize about."

I didn't wait to see if a bigger hint was coming.

"I'm *so* sorry," I said. "I can see now that what I did was horrible, and I feel awful about it, but I swear I never meant any of it the way it turned out."

My apology met with very little enthusiasm. No one threw their arms around me and told me I was forgiven, although Bill and Glenda each offered a quick, silent nod. A moment later they said they'd be going.

"Of course, we understand that one of us will have to switch out of the group," Bill told Dad. "We'll be in touch to discuss what would be best."

I was trembling inside after they left. This was easily the worst thing I'd ever done, and I didn't know what kind of punishment to expect.

At first, all I got was silence. Silence as we left, silence on the drive home, silence going into the house. By then, I couldn't take it. I started to cry.

"I really *am* sorry," I sobbed. "And I know I deserve to be grounded, and whatever other punishment you think I should get. But please, *talk* to me."

"Well, Zoey, it wasn't my intention to give you the silent treatment," he said at last. "I've been thinking about how much more serious this could have been. These people trust me. They've come to me for help."

I hung my head, ashamed.

"I could have lost two clients because of your actions. There could even have been legal issues," Dad continued. "So, as you can see, it wasn't easy, trying to decide what to do."

"But did you?" I asked. "Decide, I mean."

"I did," he said. "And you'll be happy to know that you aren't grounded."

"I'm *not?*"

"No."

I felt a rush of joy and relief. And love. Love for my wonderful, forgiving, understanding father. But he wasn't quite finished talking.

"However, you *are* fired."

Twenty-Four

I can't say it felt good to get fired from my first job. Not that I was upset with my dad. I knew he had to do what he did. But I was still pretty miserable, and I was definitely going to miss the money.

Bean wasn't exactly sympathetic after I'd (reluctantly) given him the details.

"Too bad nobody recorded any of your crackpot performances for YouTube," he said.

I ignored that and asked if Mariska was there. She was, and, after another annoying comment or two, he passed her his phone.

"Look at the good parts," Mariska said after we'd talked for a few minutes. "You aren't stuck in the house until you graduate from high school, which is about how long my parents would ground me if I did something that terrible. And your dad isn't dating his patient after all."

"You're right, and you know what? You just reminded me of something!" I told her. "I've got to go. And thanks!"

Dad was in the living room, reading something on his tablet. I noticed that his face looked tired. When I went into the room he stopped what he was doing and turned to me. I almost lost my nerve and had to take a deep breath before I could speak.

"Can I ask you something?"

"Of course."

"Who were you seeing, if it wasn't Glenda?"

"*Seeing* is hardly the right word. As I told you before, we spent some time together, very casually, and that was all."

I waited. Considering the trouble I was in, it didn't seem like a smart idea to give him a hard time, but I wasn't quite convinced. Who invites a woman to his home and makes her dinner if they're not dating?

"Anyway, I don't suppose it will do any harm to tell you, especially if that will keep you from jumping to any more wild conclusions."

Warmth crept into my cheeks as I waited.

"It sounds a bit cliché," Dad said finally, "but it was Gina."

I mustn't have looked any more enlightened, because after another pause he added, "Gina Barducci."

It still took me a few seconds to put it together.

"Miss Barducci? Your *receptionist?*" That came out louder than I intended, which startled Dad into dropping his tablet. It landed on the carpet with a soft *thunk*, and as he bent down to retrieve it, I worked at getting the horrified look off my face.

My father and his receptionist? It wasn't possible. Not that she isn't nice—she *is*. When she showed me the job, she was friendly and patient. But girlfriend material—for my dad? I have to say, absolutely not.

The best way I can sum up Miss Barducci is to tell you she's the opposite of my mom. Not just in the way she looks, either. Mom is smart and funny and interesting. I don't know if Miss Barducci is smart or not, but she's boring, and her sense of humour is the kind that's hard to figure out. She's one of those people who laugh at odd things while you force yourself to smile out of politeness.

On the plus side, she has no kids. I don't know much more about her than that. No, that's not quite true. I remember, quite a long time ago, Dad telling me that she'd been engaged when she was younger, but her fiancé died in an avalanche on a skiing trip with friends.

I realized, as these thoughts ran through my head, that Dad had scooped his tablet off the floor and was now looking at me again. "Before you leap into action, Zoey, you'll be happy to know I've made a firm decision not to pursue this, and Gina agrees it would have been a bad idea."

I almost said, "Good!" Almost. Luckily, I remembered what Mom had said about not interfering in my dad's life. And *that* reminded me I had something else to clear up.

Dad didn't say much when I told him that Ray was the one who had broken up with Mom, instead of the other way around. In fact, his only response was, "I see." Then he asked me if I had any homework, which I took as a hint that he'd like a bit of time to himself. Probably to wonder where he'd gone wrong and why his daughter was such a screw-up.

Exhaustion hit me a little while later and I crawled into bed, glad the day was over and, oddly, almost happy that everything had blown up the way it had. It had gotten to be way too much. I'd become like a mad juggler, trying to keep all those secrets and strategies from slipping and falling into the wrong hands. Now, I could simply let it all go.

The last thought I had before sleep was that it would be awesome if Friday was a drama-free day.

It seemed as though I'd gotten my wish. Friday slid by like hundreds of other school days. Classes, lunch, classes, home. No hallway histrionics, no moments when I was cornered by lies or tight spots or random-acts-gone-wrong. It was just a boring, everyday kind of day ... and it was wonderful!

The call that shattered that illusion came from Jenna a few minutes after I'd made it home from school. Even though her words were even, I could hear the fear and panic in her voice.

"Something terrible has happened," she told me. "I'm coming over. I'll tell you everything when I get there. In the meantime, call Bean and get him to meet us at your place, pronto." Here, her voice broke and she barely managed to add, "I don't know what I'm going to do."

I made the call she'd asked me to.

"Mariska's with me," Bean said. "Should I bring her?"

"Of course," I said, without hesitation. "She's one of us now."

Jenna was at my door in no time, pale and trembling. Her backpack was still hanging from her shoulder, which told me she'd come straight from school. I ushered her inside and steered her to the couch before asking her what was going on.

"We have to wait for Bean," she answered. The thin hold she had on her emotions let go then and she burst into wrenching sobs.

My alarm was growing so it was a relief to see Bean and Mariska at the door only moments later. Bean watched, looking worried, while Mariska and I did our best to calm Jenna. Eventually, she pulled herself together enough to speak, but none of us could possibly have prepared ourselves for what she said.

"I think I might have killed someone."

You would expect a statement like that to bring an onslaught of questions, wouldn't you? Like, "Who'd you kill?" and "Why?" for example. So it was kind of strange that nobody said a word. I guess we were too shocked to speak. I felt my mouth go dry while my heart started to race.

"I think I killed Ms. Preston!"

Ms. Preston is one of Breval Middle School's best history teachers. The crazy thought struck me that Jenna could have made a better choice.

"Ms. *Preston?*" Mariska's face drained to a pasty white. "You *can't* be serious."

"What happened?" I asked, finally finding my voice.

"It was my random act of kindness," Jenna said miserably.

"Not exactly the kindest thing any of us have done," Bean observed.

We glared at him.

"This is hardly the time for jokes, Bean," Mariska said.

"Sorry," he said. "Nervous reaction."

"*You're* nervous!" Jenna cried. "*I'm* the one who killed Ms. Preston!"

"Okay, you really have to stop saying that!" Bean put his hands up, like a mime pretending to push against a wall.

"You don't *know*. Not for sure—right?" I said.

"It didn't look good," Jenna moaned.

"What happened? Exactly?" Bean asked.

"I was peer-tutoring Claire Dion after classes today when all of a sudden we heard a ruckus in the hallway. Running, yelling ... we went to see what was going on and there were emergency workers carrying a stretcher ... with Ms. Preston on it!"

That was as far as Jenna got before she lost it and began sobbing again. I did my best to calm her, and eventually she managed to get more of the story out.

"I should *never* have put the teachers' cookies in that container yesterday! Because I was rushing, I forgot to switch the label with the list of ingredients. The first batch was sugar cookies, but the ones I brought yesterday had chopped walnuts in them."

"And you think that's what, ki ... uh, made Ms. Preston sick?" I said.

Jenna nodded miserably. "After the ambulance took her, I remembered that she told the class one time that she had some serious allergies. I bet nuts is one of them."

I struggled to remind myself that Jenna was only guessing. Maybe none of this had anything to do with her cookies. But no matter how much I wanted to believe that, I had to admit there was a chance that she was right and Ms. Preston had taken a deadly bite of the mislabelled cookies.

"Anaphylactic shock," Mariska said.

"What?" Jenna asked.

"That's what it's called—when someone has a severe allergic reaction to something."

I remembered hearing stories of people dying just from putting something they were allergic to in their mouths. Even spitting it out hadn't helped because their throats had swollen shut and, unable to breathe, they died before help could reach them.

"Did you get a good look?" I asked Jenna.

"At what?"

"At Ms. Preston. When they were taking her out of the school."

"Not really. There were people around, and they had the ambulance backed right up to the door, so there wasn't much chance to see her. Why?"

I shook my head and shrugged, like it was nothing. There was no point in getting into it until we knew more, but if Ms. Preston had been having difficulty breathing, that might be proof that the problem was indeed an allergic reaction. On the other hand, if there was no sign of trouble in that area, we could all relax.

Since Jenna hadn't seen her, there was no way of knowing either way.

My attention was pulled away from these thoughts by a fresh outburst of sobbing. Bean put an arm around Jenna's shoulders, a bit awkwardly, and made a comment that I didn't find particularly helpful.

"Well, in any case," he said, "you didn't mean to do it."

I plunked down beside them and cleared my throat.

Actually, I had to clear it a few times—getting a bit louder with each repeat—before it penetrated the fresh wails.

"Okay, Jenna, you need to calm down," I said sternly. "We have to find out what happened—not just what *might* have happened—before we go off the deep end here."

"Go easy on her," Bean said, casting an indignant look in my direction. "After all, she could be going to, to *jail* ... for *murder*."

"No one is going to jail for murder," I said, wondering why some people's brains seemed to stop functioning at times like this. "We don't know for sure if Ms. Preston had an allergic reaction. Maybe she twisted her ankle or something."

"But it *could* have been my cookies." Jenna sniffed. I was encouraged to see that she seemed to be calming down a little.

"Even if it was," I said, "it might not have been as serious as you think."

"And anyway, no one knows whose cookies they were," Bean added. "We just have to make sure we get that container out of there before anyone makes the connection."

"How would they know it was Jenna's anyway—even if it was still there?" Mariska asked.

"They could fingerprint it," Bean said.

"*All* of our fingerprints are on that container!" I said.

Jenna looked horrified. "You guys! This isn't about getting away with something. I would have to turn myself in, even if they didn't figure it out."

"But you aren't *really* guilty," Bean said. "It's not like you *meant* to kill her."

I spoke up quickly before Bean's words could set Jenna off again. "Can we worry about this once we actually *know* what's going on?"

"How are we going to find out?" Jenna said.

"We'll go to the hospital," I told her, "and ask."

"Ask if she's still alive?"

"No. We'll just ask for her room number. That's got to tell us something helpful—like if she's in a regular room or intensive care or whatever."

So we all put on brave faces and prepared ourselves to find out whether Jenna had just killed off a teacher with her random act.

Of kindness.

Twenty-Five

Bean called a cab and we got to the hospital about ten minutes later. Inside, we hurried to the information desk. The woman on duty gave us a once-over like it didn't matter to her if we knew she was sizing us up. Her name tag identified her as S. Shapiro.

"Yes?" she said at last.

"Uh, hi. Could you tell us where Ms. Preston is?" Bean asked.

"There's a limit for visitors," S. Shapiro said. "Two at a time."

"We're not here to visit," Bean said.

"Then why do you want to know where she is?" Her tone was instantly suspicious, which matched the way her eyes narrowed as she looked us over more carefully. Maybe S. Shapiro was under the impression that she'd been hired to weed out dubious characters and not to direct visitors to patients' rooms.

Jenna burst into tears. Again.

"I mean, *she* wants to visit," Bean said. He lowered his voice and nodded toward Jenna. "The rest of us just came along to support her."

"What was the name again?" S. Shapiro asked. Her expression had softened ever so slightly.

"Preston."

"First name?"

We looked at each other.

"Ms.," said Bean after a few seconds. "I mean, she's just 'Ms.' to us. She's a teacher at our school."

"I usually have first and last names," S. Shapiro commented, but she tapped at the keyboard in front of her. Then she frowned.

"I don't see anyone by that name."

"Can you double-check?" I asked. "It's spelled P-R-E-S-T-O-N."

"It's really important," Mariska added.

Polished fingernails clicked away on the keys again but the results were the same. There was no Preston listed as a patient.

"What if she was in the morgue?" Bean asked. "Would that show up on your search?"

Jenna's sobs stopped abruptly. She stared at Bean, her eyes wide with shock.

"Is this some kind of a prank?" S. Shapiro demanded. Then, without waiting for an answer, she said, "Look, you kids had better get out of here before I call security."

We didn't wait to be told twice.

Back at my place, we did our best to keep Jenna calm while we tried to figure out what to do next. After a lot of bickering, we managed to come up with—nothing. Not a single idea, unless you want to count Bean's suggestions, which included sneaking into the morgue (like we even knew where the morgue was) and calling the police.

"What are we going to say to the police, Bean?" I asked. "'Have you had any homicides-by-cookie today?'"

Dad, who was home when we got back from the hospital, picked up immediately on the fact that something was off. He interrupted twice, once to ask if we were hungry (no one was), and then a second time fifteen minutes later to tell us we must be hungry by now, and would we like a pizza?

"Who could eat at a time like this?" Jenna blurted.

"Is there anything I can help with?" Dad asked. He looked concerned, but only mildly. He probably thought it was a boyfriend problem.

"No one can help," Jenna said, her voice heavy with despair.

"Well, I'm here if anyone needs me. Or if you kids decide you want something to eat."

"Thanks, Dad." I turned to Jenna as soon as he was out of sight. "You'd better stay here tonight. If you go home, you're going to say something to your parents, and that will only make things worse."

"Fine," she mumbled. In spite of her grumpy tone, she looked relieved.

In the background, a shadow passed over Mariska's face, and I knew instinctively that she was feeling left out, even though she forced a smile as soon as she noticed me watching her.

"You too, Mariska," I said. "We'll kick Bean out and have a girls' night."

"Is there going to be pizza first?" Bean asked. "I think I should be fed before I'm sent off to wander the streets a broken and lonely man."

"Oh, Bean," Mariska said sweetly, "you don't have to do that."

"I don't?"

"Of course not. You can just go home."

While Bean lunged at Mariska (supposedly to

teach her a lesson, but more likely as an excuse to do a little friendly wrestling), Jenna laughed for the first time since she'd discovered that she might have committed murder by walnut.

I suppose that sounds a bit blasé, which isn't how I really felt. Of course I wanted Ms. Preston to be okay. She's one of the good ones. But it all still seemed unreal. I couldn't quite believe that one of our random acts had ended in a tragedy that huge. Also, and I'm not proud of this, it had crossed my mind that, if this turned out to be true, it meant someone else's good deed had messed up *way* worse than any of mine. And that was saying something.

With the mood lightened a little, we made up our minds to put the whole horrid business out of our heads until the next day. By then, if there was any news, the gossip should have reached us. If not, we'd try to think of some other way to find out.

We gave in about the pizza before Bean left. We even walked him home after we'd all finished eating. Bean complained that the only reason we did that was because Jenna and Mariska had to stop by their places anyway, to ask about sleeping over and pick up what they needed for the night.

"Nobody likes a whiner, Bean," Mariska told him. I was liking her more all the time.

Once we'd left the duly reprimanded Bean at his place, Jenna suggested we take a long route back to my house. It was a nice evening, crisp and cool and perfect for a relaxing walk—especially after the trauma we'd just suffered through.

We made our way along Hill Street, where we passed the Midtown strip mall before crossing Milton Avenue and coming to one of the town's drugstores. In the parking lot, we saw an elderly woman carrying several bags toward her car. This gave Mariska an idea.

"Hey! What a great chance to do a random act of kindness," she said. "I'll be right back."

Jenna and I stood watching as she hurried toward the woman, who was struggling along with her purchases.

Mariska got to the woman and greeted her with a friendly, "Hi there! I'd be happy to help you with some of these." She reached out and took two bags, easily lifting them from the woman's hands.

"Which car is yours, ma'am?" she asked.

Instead of answering, the woman squared off, swung her purse through the air and slammed it into the side of Mariska's head. She would have dealt a second blow if Mariska hadn't taken a shocked step backward. The next thing, the old woman had reached into her purse and pulled out some kind of gadget. She pressed a button on it and a shrill alarm pierced the air. Not satisfied with the racket *that* made, she began yelling, "Help! Thief!" in a high, wavering voice.

"I just wanted to help you carry your bags to your car!" Mariska shouted back, but it was clear the woman wasn't listening. Mariska gave up, put the bags down and bolted back to where Jenna and I were still standing.

"This is crazy," she gasped, "but we'd better get out of here before this gets any worse."

We all turned and ran, racing through the streets until we felt we'd put enough distance between us and the scene in the parking lot.

"I can't believe she thought I was robbing her," Mariska said when we stopped to catch our breath on the cement steps of an old stone building.

Considering all the ways my own random acts had gone wrong, I had absolutely no trouble believing it.

Twenty-Six

Jenna was, quite frankly, a basket case when there was no news by the next morning. She started driving Mariska and me nuts from the moment we woke up, crying and moaning and saying the same things over and over. Did we think Ms. Preston was dead? She hated herself. Why hadn't we heard anything? How could she have been so careless? Everyone was going to shun her when they found out what she'd done. And on and on.

It was lucky that my dad was doing weekend errands. If he'd been home, we'd never have hidden from him the fact that this was no typical teen problem.

None of the things we'd said or done to calm Jenna the evening before were working anymore. I could practically see Mariska asking herself why she'd wanted to stay over, and I tried not to look at her actions as traitorous when Bean stopped by to claim her before lunch and she was out the door like a shot.

Still, that might have been for the best, because once it was just the two of us, I was finally able to get through to Jenna. Or maybe she'd just worn herself out. Either way, she calmed down and seemed to regain some control over her outbursts. Most importantly, she promised she could hold on until we found out what had happened to Ms. Preston.

She left not long after that, and I have to admit it was a relief to close the door with her on the other side.

Dad got back home about an hour later. By that time I'd cleaned up the kitchen, straightened up my room and was in the middle of sorting out the laundry. I knew it would take a while, but I was determined to prove myself to him again.

I was downstairs putting a load of clothes in the washer when Dennis called.

After staring at his number for a second, I took a deep breath and answered, "Whatever it is, yes, I probably did it."

If that threw him off, he recovered fast. "Actually, I'm doing my interrogations in person these days. Can I come over later?"

"You want to come here? To my place?"

"If it's okay, yeah."

I was tempted to ask him why, but all I said was that I'd have to check and call him back.

When I asked Dad, he cranked out a bunch of questions that were way too organized to be coming off the top of his head. They started with: "How old is this young man? What grade is he in? How long have you known him?"

Once he got past the basics, there were a few questions that were probably designed to trick me. Like: "When he gets in trouble at school, is he respectful about accepting the consequences?" (Correct answer: Actually, I don't think he's ever been in trouble at school.)

It was easy to imagine poor old Dad writing these up—a boyfriend screening list—congratulating himself for being prepared for when the time came, and thinking he could pull it off without looking rehearsed. Which he totally did.

I must have answered everything to his satisfaction because when he was done he said Dennis could come over. I let Dennis know and commenced to drive myself crazy wondering what this strange turn of events meant.

At dinner, Dad asked, "What time is your young man coming by?"

"Around 7:00, and please don't call him 'your young man' when he's here."

"Gotcha. I'll call him your beau instead."

"Dad!"

He laughed and leaned forward to pat my hand and make one of his unrelated-to-the-moment nurturing statements. This one was, "You know, Zoey, in spite of occasional missteps, you're really a good girl."

"You're a good dad, too," I said, "even if you did fire me."

Dennis's brother dropped him off a few minutes before 7:00. When I opened the door to let Dennis in, Gary beeped and gave me a thumbs-up from the driveway. I smiled and waved until Dennis was inside and the door was closed.

That was when I noticed he was holding something behind his back. When I got a peek at it, it looked like a flower, but when he brought it around and held it out to me, I saw that it was actually made of paper—and not very well, either.

"Uh, thanks," I said, taking it.

"You're welcome." He gave me a huge smile. "I made it myself."

That explained why it was such a lousy job. What I didn't get was why he'd made it in the first place. That seemed odd, which made me take a closer look. I saw that there were lines on the paper that the flower was fashioned from, but, with all the folds and creases, it took me a second or two to recognize them as bits of handwriting.

A heartbeat later I realized what I was holding, and I flung it away from me as though it had burst into flame.

"My notes!" I said.

"I thought you might like them back."

"But ... you said you gave them to Amanda."

"Actually, I rewrote them for Amanda." Dennis bent to pick up the flower and passed it back to me. "I thought you'd probably like to get the originals back."

"So, you knew the truth, even before you asked me." I couldn't bring myself to look him in the eye.

"That your writing matched the writing on the quiz? I was pretty sure, yeah."

"So, why did you bother calling to ask me?"

"I wanted to know if you'd tell me the truth."

I let that sink in for a second, then said, "I can explain about the quiz. How it happened, I mean."

"I'm listening."

So I told him how Jenna and Bean and I

had been clowning around, and how Jenna had forgotten all about it by the time she decided to take the magazines to school. For good measure, I went ahead and filled him in about our pledge to do random acts of kindness, and how that had all started when Destiny said Bean wasn't welcome in the Lend a Hand club.

"I never thought anyone else would ever see that quiz—I wouldn't do anything that mean," I finished.

"That's why I'm here—I just couldn't believe you'd do something so deliberately malicious." Dennis took a step closer to me, which made my heart rev into overdrive. But something outside the window caught his attention.

"Um, there's a police car pulling into your driveway," he told me.

"The police?" I said. Then a jolt of shock and horror hit me. I hadn't heard from Jenna since she'd left, but it didn't take much brain-power to guess what had happened. She must have found out that her cookies really *had* killed Ms. Preston, and she'd turned herself in.

I told myself that the police were here to talk to me as part of their investigation, but I knew it might be more serious than that. It was possible that Jenna had said something to implicate the rest of us. Not on purpose, of course—she would never do that—but if she was flustered, who knows what she might have blurted out?

The officer knocked before I had a chance to gather my thoughts. When I opened the door he glanced at his notepad and said, "Are you Zoey Dalton?"

"Yes, sir."

"I believe you've been expecting me. Is that right?"

"Sort of," I said. "I was hoping you wouldn't need to come."

The officer took another quick look at his notes then, and while he did that I decided to go ahead and show him I was being co-operative, and that I had nothing to hide.

"I know this doesn't make it better, but what happened was totally an accident," I said.

The officer gave me a strange look. "I don't see how it could have been an accident," he said.

"But it *was*," I insisted. "The three of us were doing random acts of kindness—well, it was three at first until Bean's girlfriend joined us. So, I guess it was actually four by the time it happened. Anyway, Jenna brought cookies but the bag broke so she had to use the plastic container again and she forgot to switch the ingredient label. That's what caused the death—but it was totally accidental. We all *like*

Ms. Preston. And Jenna would never hurt anyone on purpose."

"Ms. Preston is *dead?*" Dennis asked from behind me.

At the very same time, the officer said, "Are you telling me that someone is dead—and one of your friends is responsible?"

"Isn't that why you're here?" I asked.

"No. I'm here following up on the theft of leaves from the Kimuras' yard up the street."

"Oh."

"I came to let you know that they're not going to press charges, but they'd like you to go and apologize to them."

"Oh. Okay. Sure—I'll be happy to do that," I said.

"Good." The officer flipped his notepad closed, but he wasn't quite finished. "Now, what was it you were saying about someone causing a death?"

I sighed. "Maybe we'd better sit down for a minute," I said.

Once we were in the living room, I told him again about the cookies, only this time in a slower version that he could follow. The officer asked me a bunch of questions and then he excused himself and went to the next room to make some phone calls in private. While he was gone I looked over at Dennis and gave him a weak smile. He looked like he might be in a bit of shock. To be completely honest, I was a bit surprised he was still there.

The officer was gone for five or ten minutes, although it felt a lot longer. He came back with a smile and the best news ever. Ms. Preston wasn't dead. The ambulance had been called for her because some heavy books she was trying to get down from a high shelf had conked her on the head.

"But we went to the hospital and they told us she wasn't there," I said.

"She was never admitted—only treated as an outpatient and released."

"That's fantastic!" I said. "Can I send Jenna a text to let her know right away? She's been a complete wreck."

The officer waited for me to do that and then, just before he left, he reminded me about apologizing to the Kimuras.

The door was hardly shut behind him when Dennis had a question for me.

"You stole someone's *leaves*?"

"It was supposed to be one of my random acts of kindness," I told him. "How was I supposed to know I picked the only house in town where they actually wanted their leaves?"

"You have to admit it's kind of funny. I mean, now that you know you're not in trouble for it."

"I guess it's a bit funny," I said. "But I know one thing—I'm never doing a random act again. Ever."

"That's too bad, because it sounds like a good idea to me," he said. "Better than the group Destiny started—though I hear that's pretty much fallen apart now anyway."

"It might *sound* good, but everything I've tried—and I mean everything—has gone wrong." I told him about some (not all—I'm not an idiot) of the other things I'd done that hadn't turned out the way they were supposed to.

"I swear, I'm jinxed," I said. "And I think I might even be bad luck to my friends' random acts. Look at what poor Jenna just went through!"

"You were *super*-cute when you were confessing to the murder," Dennis said, making air quotes for "the murder." He tried, but failed, to keep a straight face.

"Shut up."

"Gary was right. You *are* interesting."

"Thanks. I guess." I met his eyes and a happy thrill ran through me.

"Hey," he said, "if you want to go now, to talk to the people whose leaves you stole, I'll go with you."

I thought that was a great idea, and a few minutes later we were on our way up the street. As we turned in toward the Kimuras' house, Dennis commented that their yard was one of the cleanest he'd ever seen. Wise guy.

I climbed the steps and rang the bell. Mr. Kimura appeared in the doorway and, when he saw that it was me, he called behind him and his wife came along and joined him. They stood close together. I thought they looked a little worried.

"I came to tell you how sorry I am for taking your leaves last weekend," I said. "I thought it would be a help to you."

"Not help," said Mrs. Kimura. She shook her head to be sure I got the message.

"Yes, well, I didn't know you wanted them or I would never have done it. So, I, uh, hope you can forgive me." I ended with a smile.

The Kimuras looked at each other. "We forgive you," Mrs. Kimura said, turning back to me. "Officer tell us, you not really bad girl. You good girl."

I beamed at her and said enthusiastically, "That's *right*. I was trying to do a good deed."

"We understand," said Mr. Kimura. "Except, your good deeds not very good."

"Well, I—"

"You stop good deeds now, please," Mrs. Kimura said.

Then they both nodded politely, stepped back and closed the door.

I'll say this much for Dennis, he managed to hold in his laughter until we were nearly back to my house. And when he finally stopped laughing he said he was sorry, even if he didn't look it.

"It's okay. And anyway, I'm glad that's done. At least now they know I'm not a psycho of some sort."

"Always a good thing to get cleared up," Dennis teased. Then he asked, "You in a hurry to get back inside?"

"Not really. Why?"

"I thought maybe we could take a walk."

And that's what we did. The evening air smelled faintly of woodsmoke and something sweet that I couldn't quite identify, and it felt wonderful to be walking along with Dennis. We'd gone a couple of blocks when he reached across the short space between us and took my hand.

"Are you really giving up on random acts of kindness?" he asked.

"I don't know. That's how I feel right now, but I suppose it could change. Anyway, the way my random acts turn out, it might actually be kinder for me *not* to do any more," I said ruefully.

Dennis laughed a little at that. Then he stopped walking, and tugged my hand to signal me to do the same. When we were both standing still on the sidewalk, he turned to face me.

I felt a tremble skitter through me as he looked deep into my eyes.

"I was just wondering, how do you feel about random acts of kissing?" he asked.

As it happened, I felt just fine about that.

Acknowledgments

A lot of people committed random acts of helpfulness during the writing and editing of this book. I'm grateful to each and every one of them.

Particular thanks to Lynne Missen for believing in the story. Your patient guidance was such a help, and most sincerely appreciated.

My husband, Brent, who supports my work in so many ways.

My family and friends—I hope you know what you mean to me.

Early on, readers from kidcrit were more than generous with their time and suggestions. Those chapter-by-chapter critiques were invaluable and encouraged me to keep on.

On the subject of random acts of kindness, I'd like to go on record as being *for* them! Sure, the characters in this story encountered some odd situations, and their random acts may have gone a tad askew, but I hope that won't discourage anyone from reaching out a helping hand. Make the world a better place.